# PHARMACOGNOSY OF TRADITIONAL DRUGS - II

## S. B. GOKHALE

M. Pharm., AIC
Former Co-ordinator,
R.C. Patel Institute of Pharmaceutical Education and Research
**Shirpur - 425405 (M.S.)**

## Dr. C. K. KOKATE

M. Pharm., Ph. D., F.G.A.E.S. (Germany)
**President,**
Indian Society of Pharmacognosy and
**Vice-chancellor,**
KLE University, JNMC Campus, Nehru Nagar,
**Belgaum - 590010 (Karnataka)**

## Dr. ALPANA GOKHALE

B.A.M.S.
Consulting Physican,
Swargate, **PUNE - 411037**

## Dr. M. G. KALASKAR

M. Pharm., Ph. D.
**Asstt. Professor**
R.C. Patel Institute of Pharmaceutical Education and Research
**Shirpur - 425405 (M.S.)**

**NIRALI PRAKASHAN**
ADVANCEMENT OF KNOWLEDGE

N1627

**Pharmacognosy of Traditional Drugs - II**   ISBN 978-93-5164-206-0

**First Edition**   : **January 2016**

©   :   **Authors**

**Published By :**

**NIRALI PRAKASHAN**

Abhyudaya Pragati, 1312, Shivaji Nagar,
Off J.M. Road, PUNE – 411005
Tel - (020) 25512336/37/39, Fax - (020) 25511379
Email : niralipune@pragationline.com

## ☞ DISTRIBUTION CENTRES

**PUNE**

Nirali Prakashan : 119, Budhwar Peth, Jogeshwari Mandir Lane, Pune 411002, Maharashtra
Tel : (020) 2445 2044, 66022708, Fax : (020) 2445 1538
Email : bookorder@pragationline.com, niralilocal@pragationline.com

Nirali Prakashan : S. No. 28/27, Dhyari, Near Pari Company, Pune 411041
Tel : (020) 24690204 Fax : (020) 24690316
Email : dhyari@pragationline.com, bookorder@pragationline.com

**MUMBAI**

Nirali Prakashan : 385, S.V.P. Road, Rasdhara Co-op. Hsg. Society Ltd.,
Girgaum, Mumbai 400004, Maharashtra
Tel : (022) 2385 6339 / 2386 9976, Fax : (022) 2386 9976
Email : niralimumbai@pragationline.com

## ☞ DISTRIBUTION BRANCHES

**JALGAON**

Nirali Prakashan : 34, V. V. Golani Market, Navi Peth, Jalgaon 425001,
Maharashtra, Tel : (0257) 222 0395, Mob : 94234 91860

**KOLHAPUR**

Nirali Prakashan : New Mahadvar Road, Kedar Plaza, 1st Floor Opp. IDBI Bank
Kolhapur 416 012, Maharashtra. Mob : 9850046155

**NAGPUR**

Pratibha Book Distributors : Above Maratha Mandir, Shop No. 3, First Floor,
Rani Jhanshi Square, Sitabuldi, Nagpur 440012, Maharashtra
Tel : (0712) 254 7129

**DELHI**

Nirali Prakashan : 4593/21, Basement, Aggarwal Lane 15, Ansari Road, Daryaganj
Near Times of India Building, New Delhi 110002
Mob : 08505972553

**BENGALURU**

Pragati Book House : House No. 1, Sanjeevappa Lane, Avenue Road Cross,
Opp. Rice Church, Bengaluru – 560002.
Tel : (080) 64513344, 64513355,Mob : 9880582331, 9845021552
Email:bharatsavla@yahoo.com

**CHENNAI**

Pragati Books : 9/1, Montieth Road, Behind Taas Mahal, Egmore,
Chennai 600008 Tamil Nadu, Tel : (044) 6518 3535,
Mob : 94440 01782 / 98450 21552 / 98805 82331,
Email : bharatsavla@yahoo.com

niralipune@pragationline.com   |   www.pragationline.com

Also find us on [f]   www.facebook.com/niralibooks

# PREFACE TO THE FIRST EDITION

We are very happy to present **"Pharmacognosy of Traditional Drugs - II"** to the students, colleagues, Ayurvedic practitioners and professionals of Traditional Drugs.

Most of the vital and essential information except microscopic characters, (which can not be practiced by actual users) is provided in the text.

We have tried to compile the recent technical information in all respects of these drugs by using all possible sources and modern techniques for traditional drug practitioners.

We hope our this attempt will satisfy the actual needs of the users.


**Dhantrayodashi**                                                              **Authors**
**09-11-2015**

# CONTENTS

1. **TERPENOIDAL DRUGS**                                              **1.1 – 1.49**
   - Anantmula                                                          1.1
   - Chandan                                                            1.4
   - Guggul                                                             1.7
   - Haridra                                                            1.11
   - Jatamansi                                                          1.15
   - Lasuna                                                             1.18
   - Maricha                                                            1.21
   - Nagarmotha                                                         1.24
   - Nirgundi                                                           1.26
   - Pipali                                                             1.29
   - Sallaki                                                            1.31
   - Sunthi                                                             1.34
   - Tamal Patra                                                        1.37
   - Tulasi                                                             1.39
   - Vacha                                                              1.41
   - Vidanga                                                            1.44
   - Musk                                                               1.48

2. **LIPIDS**                                                          **2.1 – 2.26**
   - Bhilama                                                            2.1
   - Castor Oil                                                         2.3
   - Cocoa Butter                                                       2.6
   - Karanja Oil                                                        2.8
   - Linseed                                                            2.10
   - Linseed Oil                                                        2.12
   - Olive Oil                                                          2.14
   - Sesame Oil                                                         2.16
   - Beeswax                                                            2.18
   - Cod Liver Oil                                                      2.20
   - Shark Liver Oil                                                    2.23
   - Wool Fat                                                           2.25

3.  **CARBOHYDRATES**                          **3.1 – 3.5**
    - Isapgol                                   3.1
    - Madhu (Mel)                               3.4
4.  **MIXED CHEMICAL CONSTITUENTS**             **4.1 – 4.36**
    - Artemisia                                 4.1
    - Bala                                      4.3
    - Benafsha                                  4.6
    - Chitrak                                   4.8
    - Colocynth                                 4.10
    - Dhataki Pushpa                            4.12
    - Kalijiri                                  4.14
    - Kushta                                    4.16
    - Malkangani                                4.19
    - Neem                                      4.22
    - Pashanbhed                                4.24
    - Parijatak                                 4.27
    - Shiwan                                    4.30
    - Vajradanti                                4.33

    **Bibliography**                            **B.1 – B.1**

    **Glossary**                                **G.1 – G.8**

    **Appendix**                                **A.1 – A.4**

    **Biological Index**                        **B.1 – B.1**

    **Synonym Index**                           **S.1 – S.1**

    **Chemical Index**                          **C.1 – C.2**

# Chapter 1

# TERPENOIDAL DRUGS

## ANANTMULA

**Synonyms**

Sariva, Indian Sarsaparilla.

**Biological Source**

It consists of dried roots of the plant known as *Hemidesmus indicus* Linn. belonging to family Asclepiadaceae. The roots contain not less than 0.020 per cent of Iso-vanillin evaluated on dry basis.

**Geographical Source**

It is found more frequently in Jharkhand, Kerala, Chhattisgarh, Karnataka and also in Sri Lanka.

**Description of Herb**

It is perennial creeper with fragment odour, stems are slender while leaves are without trichomes dark green colour, with whitish patches of 5 - 10 cm long 0.5 - 5.0 cm wide, flowers are greenish, in clusters, fruits are 10 - 15 cm long, green, narrow cylindrical with pointed tips and are present in pairs seeds are small, black with a bunchy of white hairs at top. It is a laticiferrous herb.

**Macroscopic Characters**

Anantmula roots are woody, thickened at nodes, leaves are opposite short and petioled, variable in size and shape. Flowers are greenish outside and purplish inside. Fruits are dehiscent follicles, about 10 cm long. Seeds are numerous, black and flattened.

**Fig. 1.1 : Indian sarsaparilla herb**

| | | |
|---|---|---|
| **Colour** | : | Roots are yellowish brown, centre or yellow surrounded by milky white cortical layer |
| **Odour** | : | Vanilline - like |
| **Taste** | : | Aromatic and sweetish |
| **Size** | : | 30 cm or more in length 3 - 6 mm in thickness. |

**Shape**          :     Cylendrical, seldom branched, having corky bark, longitudinal furrows and transverse fissures. All plants have white milky juice.

**Fracture**      :     Short at periphery and fibrous in the centre.

**Extra Features :** Roots are branched provided with few thick rootlets and secondary roots with marked transverse cracks and longitudinal fissures easily detachable from the hand central core.

## Chemical Constituents

Roots contain about 0.2 per cent vol. oil. Roots also contain β sitosterol, α and β amyrins, lupeol, tannins and saponin. Sarsasapogenin. Sarsasaponin contain 3 glucose and one rhamnose as sugar components.

**Sarsapogenin**                                   **Hemidesminine**

Volatile oil containing p-methothy salicylic acehyde as major constituent. Roots contain coumarino-lignoids, Hemidesminine and hemidesmin I, hemidesmin II. Iso vanilline is the main constituent responsible for pleasant flavour of the drug.

## Standards of Quality

(1)  Foreign organic matter          :  Not more than 2.0 per cent

(2)  Alcohol soluble extractives     :  Not less than 8.0 per cent

(3)  Water soluble extractives       :  Not less than 12.0 per cent

(4)  Ash contents                    :  Not more than 15.0 per cent

(5)  Acid insoluble ash              :  Not less than 02.0 per cent

(6)  Loss on drying                  :  Not less than 12.0 per cent by using 5 gm in an oven at 105°C.

## Ayurvedic Properties

1.  Rasa      :  Madhur, tikta

2.  Guna      :  Snigdha

3.  Veerya    :  Sheet

4.  Vipak     :  Madhura

## Uses

Syrup of the root is used as flavouring agent and in preparation of herbal tea. It is also used a blood purifier, in rheumatism, anti-inflammatory tonic in urinary disorders. Powdered roots are used for pre and post natal care, and to increase lactation in cows. It is used in psoriasis and also a flavour in beverages.

## Traditional Uses

- It is one of the Rasayana plants of Ayurveda used as alternative, febrifuge, diuretic, anti-inflammatory, antimiscarriage, fertility tonic.

- It is used in eczema, psoriasis urticaria, acen - it clears the blood reduces lymphatic swellings, stops itching and reduces inflammation, stop itching and reduces suppuration.

- It is used as an external paste or as a cream to benefit the above skin problems.

- Root powder useful in STD.

- It is useful in cystitis, urethritis, kidney infections, prostatis.

- It stimulates appetite in pita prakurti without aggravating any acidity.

- It is useful in diseases of bone and joint i.e. as anti-inflammatory in arthritis and gout.

- It is used in disturbed and irritated emotions as anxiolytic.

- In gynaecology it is useful to main pregnancy and prevent habitual miscarriage.

- It is an important ingredients in several classical ayurvedic formulation e.g. Pinda taila.

## Storage

Protect the drug against insect and rodent attack and keep away from moisture and heat.

## Market Formulations

1. **Panda taila :** Aathreya Ayurveda Pharma No. 53/6, Kaveripura Magadi main road, Kamakshipalya Bengaluru - 560079.

2. **Sarivadyasava :** Dabur India, Gaziabad 201010, UP.

# CHANDAN

## Synonyms

White Saunders, Yellow saunders.

## Biological Source

It is the heart wood of plant *Sanitalum album* belonging to family Santalaceae.

## Geographical Source

It is found widely distributed in India, mainly in Mysore, Coorg, Coimbatore, Nilgiris, Andhra Pradesh, Bihar, Gujarat, Karnataka, Madhya Pradesh, Maharashtra and Tamil Nadu.

## Description of Herb

Chandan is a small, evergreen, 10 - 14 mts high a partial root parasitic plant.

## Bark

Its outer side is black brown, internally it is reddish. Surface is rough with vertical cracks.

## Heart Wood

The sap wood whitish and odourless, while the heart wood is yellowish or pale red in colour. It is very much dense and hard, containing higher oil concentration highly scented.

## Leaves

Leaves are 2.5 to 6 cm long, oblong, dark green and shining on the upper surface.

## Flowers

Flowers are small yellowish with purple tinge appearing in bunches.

## Fruits

Small, roundish with 1 cm diameter, green turning black at maturity.

## Types

Shwet Chandan and Rakta chandan are two types.

## Useful Parts

Heart wood and volatile oil.

## Cultivation

Cultivation of the drug is done by sowing seeds. The seed are raised on nursery bed and than transplanted. Chandan is of parasitic nature, hence they grows along with the supports of host plant. It is harvested at the age of 30 to 40 years.

## Collection

Chandan is slow growing tree for obtaining heartwood, it attains maturity at the age of 50 to 60 years. The full mature plants are uprooted. The bark from roots and stem is removed the heartwood is separated. It is cut into pieces.

Volatile oil extracted from the heart wood is stored in well closed containers away from sunlight in dark place.

## Macroscopic Characters

| | | |
|---|---|---|
| **Colour** | : | Pale yellow to reddish yellow in colour |
| **Odour** | : | Characteristic, persistant |
| **Taste** | : | Bitter |
| **Size** | : | Cutouts of heartwood of various size and shape |

**Fig. 1.2 : Sandal wood plant**

## Volatile Oil :

| | | |
|---|---|---|
| **Colour** | : | Pale yellow to colourless viscid liquid |
| **Odour** | : | Characteristic, persistant |
| **Taste** | : | Unpleasant |
| **Solubility** | : | Slightly soluble in water and soluble in alcohol, chloroform, propylene, glycol, mineral oil and fixed oils. It is insoluble in glycerine. |

## Chemical Constituents

It contains two sesquiterpene alcohol, $\alpha$-santalol and $\beta$-santalol, resin, tannic acid, santenone, teresantol, santalone, esters, free acid, aldehyde santalal.

$\alpha$**-Santalol**                          $\beta$**-Santalol**

## Standards of Quality :

**Sandal Wood Oil**

| | | |
|---|---|---|
| **Density** | : | 0.965 - 0.980 at 25° |
| **Refractive Index :** | | 1.500 - 1.510 |

## Pharmacological Uses

It shows cooling, sedative and astringent action. It also shows diuretic, expectorant and stimulant action. In the treatment of urinary tract inflammations. Oil is used in perfumes, and as fragrance increams and lotions.

## Ayurvedic Properties

| | | |
|---|---|---|
| **Rasa** | : | Tikta |
| **Veepak** | : | Katu |
| **Veerya** | : | Sheeta |
| **Guna** | : | Laghu, Rooksha |
| **Doshagnatha** | : | Pittaghna, Kaphaghava, Vaatkar |

## Traditional Uses

(a) Chandan oil alongwith lemon juice is applied in scabies.

(b) Along with rice water it is given in case of urinary incontinence and dysentery.

(c) Wood powder in coconut water is administerial in thirst.

(d) In diabetes, leucorrthia, alongwith cardamom powder chandan oil.

(e) To subside heat, chandan powder alongwith kapoor and vittiver powder applied externally.

## Dosage

| | | |
|---|---|---|
| **Powder** | : | 1 to 3 grams |
| **Volatile oil** | : | 5 to 20 drops |

## Substitutes

(a) Volatile oil obtained from *Eucarya spicata,* known as Australian Sandal wood oil is substituted.

(b) Oil obtained from *Ampris balsamifera* is used as substitute to sandalwood oil.

## Adulterants

Volatile oil is often adulterated with fixed oils.

## Storage

**Oil :** It should be stored in well-filled, well closed containers away from sunlight in cool place.

**Sandal Wood :** Cut pieces of heart wood of sandal are dumped in soil for few days and thenthey are removed, cleaned and stored in dark place away from sunlight.

## Market Formulation

1. **Sunscreen Lotion :** V.L.C.C. Personal Care Ltd., Plot No. 11 & 12 Sec. - 6A, Sidkul, IIE, Haridwar, Uttarakhand - 249403.

2. **Mysore Sandal Soap :** Karnataka Soaps & Detergents Ltd., 27, Industrial suburb, Bangalore - Pune Highway, Rajaji Nagar, Bangalore - 560055.

3. **Chandanadi Churna :** Chandanadivati, Chandanasar, Shadangodak, Chandanba-lakshaditaila.

# GUGGUL

Over 2,000 years ago the ancient Sanskrit medical texts mentioned the resin from *Commiphora mukul* as "clearing the coating and obstruction of channels", which was their way of talking about clogged arteries from rich food. They also used this for obesity, acne vulgaris, diarrhea, arthritis, rheumatism, and urinary problems. This resin has been a part of Ayurvedic medicine for twenty centuries, but has only recently been discovered in the West. Finally an ancient and established herbal tradition has been validated by western science.

## Synonyms

Guggule, Gugal, Gum gugal, Bdellium.

## Biological Source

It consists of exudates/oleogum resin obtained after incision on the stems of plant *Commiphora mukul* (Hooker, stedor) Engl. (*Balsamodendron mukul* hook) family: Burseracae.

## Geographical Source

It is native of Africa, specially Ethophia, Somalia Kenya and Zimbabwe.

Guggul has been a key component in ancient Indian Ayurvedic system of medicine. But has become so scarce because of its overuse in its two habitats in India where it is found – Gujarat and Rajasthan that the World Conservation Union (IUCN) has enlisted it in its Red Data List of endangered species.

When used for medicinal purposes, the resin, harvested from the stems in the winter, is traditionally processed to purify and render it bioassimilable by placing the gum into a bag of thick, coarse cloth and then boiling it in an aqueous medium such as pure water or a decoction of Triphala until it is soft. This is then spread out and on a wooden board where it is smeared with ghee (clarified butter) and allowed to air dry. The dried gum is again fried in ghee and finely powdered for medicinal use.

## Description of Herb

**Plant:** It is a shrub or small tree, reaching a maximum height of 4 m, with thin papery bark. The branches are thorny. The leaves are simple or trifoliate, the leaflets ovate, 1-5 cm long, 0.5-2.5 cm broad, irregularly toothed. It is gynodioecious, with some plants bearing bisexual and male flowers, and others with female flowers. The individual flowers are red to pink, with four small petals.

## Macroscopy Characters

| | | |
|---|---|---|
| **Color** | : | Brown |
| **Odour** | : | Arromatic, Balsamic |
| **Taste** | : | Bitter |
| **Size** | : | Varing sizes |
| **Shape** | : | Tears |
| **Extra feature** | : | Tears are mixed with pieces of bark. When triturated with water it produces milky emulsion. Sticky, brittle in nature, fracture short. |

**Fig. 1.3 : Commophora - mukul herb**

## Chemical Composition

It is a complex mixture of organic and inorganic constituents. It is mixture of essential oil, gum and resinous substances. The essential oil content found to content maximum uo to 11%. Large number of steroids have been isolated from oleogum resin. The z guggulosterone and E guggulosterol, I, II and III are bioactive. Recently partial synthesis of guggulosterol II from diosgenin has been reported. Additionally, combrene A and mubulol a diterpene constituent are also reported.

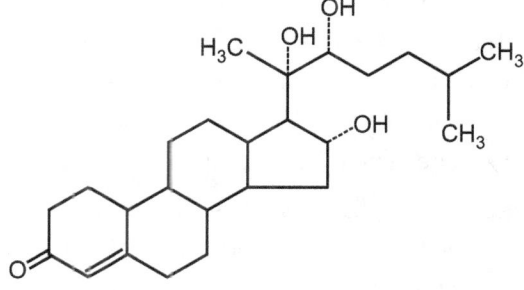

          **Guggulosterone - z**                 **Guggulosterol I**

## Standards of Quality

| | |
|---|---|
| Ash value | ⅍ 5.5 percent |
| Acid insoluble ash | ⅍ 3.5 percent |
| Loss on drying | ⅍ 11.8 percent |
| Water soluble extractive | ⅍ 48.0 percent |
| Alcohol soluble extractive | ⅍ 40.0 percent |

## Ayurvedic Properties

| | | |
|---|---|---|
| **Rasa** | : | Tikta, katu, madhu, kasaya |
| **Guna** | : | Laghu, teekshna, snigdha, pichila, sar. |
| **Veerya** | : | Ushna |
| **Vipak** | : | Katu |

## Uses

## Pharmacological Uses:

- The oleoresin shown to posses highly potent anti-inflammatory effect as good as hydrocortisone.
- In experimental animal, exhibited strong antihyperlipidemic activity.
- In chronic endometritis, amenorrhea and menorrhagia it is particularly valued.
- In clinical studies, it was found to improve the condition of leprosy patient, relives lassitude, relieves nervous pains and gives the sense of well being.

- Scientists have found, that guggul reduces platelet stickiness so overclotting does not occur in the blood, which causes strokes and heart attacks.

- A study in 1988 (Planta Medica, volume 4) showed guggul also stimulates thyroid metabolism and function. Increasing metabolism efficiency of the thyroid gland can mean losing weight without eating less.

- A study in France was reported in Rombi's Phytotherapy, A Practical Handbook of Herbal Medicine (1988) showing guggul could lower levels of uric acid in the blood i.e. useful in gout. In fact a study in the Journal of the American Medical Association in 2000 (volume 283, pages 2404-10) found that uric acid levels studied in 5,926 people is an accurate predictor of ischemic heart disease and mortality. They said, "for each increase in uric acid level, cardiovascular mortality and ischemic heart disease increased." So, guggul has other heart healthy advantages than just lowering cholesterol and triglyceride levels.

- 25 mg of guggul sterones lower cholesterol are by binding bile acids in the intestine, stimulating fat digesting enzymes (lipases), and inhibiting what is called "HMG-CoA" reductase enzymes in the liver which help support cholesterol production. Guggul therefore has several mechanisms of action which lower our blood fats.

- In clinical studies it was found that 14-27% fall in cholesterol levels and an 22 - 30% fall in triglyceride levels in only 90 days or less when guggul was given to men and women with high blood lipid profiles. The mechanism thought to be responsible for this kind of effectiveness is that guggul stimulates the liver to take up more of the LDL cholesterol from the blood and destroy it. Lower LDL levels are always better.

## Traditional Uses

Tridosh har, soth har, badana samak, barn shodhan, hirdya, mutral, kutaghn, dipan, arsoghona, rasayana. Used in all tyoes of vat *bayadh.*

*According to Bhava Prakasha*

- **New Guggul:** It has comparatively less tendency for reducing obesity. This is smooth, golden in color, fragrant, sticky and like ripe Jamun or Jamun (*Syzygium cumini*) fruit.

- **Old Guggul:** This has greater tendency to reduce weight and burn fat. This form is dry, with unpleasant odor, and without much medicinal property. It should only be used for reducing weight.

## Therapeutic Uses :

- It is an astringent and antiseptic in abraded or broken skin.
- It has appetizing, carminative, anti suppurative, aphrodisiac and emmenagogue properties.
- It is used as anti- cholesterolemic, anti-platelet agent.
- As an Anti arthritic and anti-inflammatory agent.
- Also useful in over weight reduction in humans i.e. anti-obesity

## Guggul in Atherveda

- Two types of this herb are described - one near the rivers and the other near the ocean.

- This herb is mentioned as fragrant and vital energy enhancing agent.

- As Vermicide or anti-helminthic and Anti-tubercular.

- It was used chiefly for sacred fire rites and for fumigation.

- It was mentioned for leucoderma (white patches of skin) and greying of hair.

- If the fragrance of fumigation this herb is smelled daily, one can boost his resistance against infections like tuberculosis. This refers to the mmuno-boosting effect of guggul.

## Ayurveda Guggul : Important points to be noted

When administering gugguly in accordance with the principles of Ayurvedic medicine, the following points must be considered:

1. Guggul resin is produced more abundantly and is stronger in potency during the season of autumn; hence, Ayurveda states that guggul resin must be collected in autumn.

2. Different selections of guggul resin have different therapeutic actions based on the age of the guggulu. Freshly collected guggulu has a Brumhana (weight increasing) quality, where as Purana guggul (guggul which is at least one year old) has an Atilekhana (weight reducing) quality.

3. **Shuddha Guggul:** Guggul has to be purified in cow's milk in order to remove toxic substances and render the guggulu easily absorbable. Ayurveda specifies Shodhana (purification) as one of the important procedures before oral administration of guggul. To purify guggul in this manner, it should be wrapped in a sack of cotton cloth and dipped in simmering cow's milk, which must be continuously stirred until all the pure substance of the guggul is absorbed into the milk. When this process is complete, the milk containing the pure guggul gum resin will be solidified and the cotton sack containing the impurities or toxins of the guggulu is to be discarded.

## Marketed Preparations

1. **Sinhnad Guggul :** Patanjali Ayurved Limited, Haridwar, Uttarakhand - 249401.

2. **Triphala guggul :** Patanjali Ayurved Limited, Haridwar, Uttarakhand - 249401.

3. **Lakshadi guggul :** Shree Baidyanath Ayurved Bhawan Pvt. Ltd, Kolkata, West Bengal.

## Adulterants

Guggul is found adulterated with resins of varcus species of Commophora as *Commiphora abyssinia*; *Commiphora roxhurgi* and *Boswellia serrata*.

# HARIDRA

Haridra (Turmeric) is a plant that has a very long history of medicinal use, dating back nearly 4000 years in India. In Southeast Asia, turmeric is used not only as a principal spice but also as a component in religious ceremonies. Because of its brilliant yellow color, turmeric is also known as "Indian saffron." Modern medicine has begun to recognize its importance, as indicated by the over 3000 publications dealing with turmeric that came out within the last 25 years.

According to Sanskrit medical treatises and Ayurvedic and Unani systems, turmeric has a long history of medicinal use in South Asia. Susruta's Ayurvedic Compendium, dating back to 250 BC, recommends an ointment containing turmeric to relieve the effects of poisoned food.

In Sanskrit, turmeric has at least 53 different names indicating their usefulness some of them are as gauri (to make fair), haldi (that draws attention to its bright color), haridra (dear to hari, Lord Krishna), hridayovilosini (gives delight to heart, charming), joyanti (one that wins over diseases), jawarantika (which cures fevers), mongolproda (who bestows auspiciousness), mangolya (auspicious), mehagni (Killer of fat), nisho (night), nishokhyo (known as night), nishawa (clears darkness and imparts color), rabhongavaso (which dissolves fat), vishogni (killer of poison), and yuvati (young girl).

## Synonyms

Turmeric, Indian Saffron, Haldi.

## Biological Source

It consists of well prepared, dried rhizomes of plant *curcuma longa* L. (family: zingiberaceae)

## Geographical Source

In India it is found almost in all states, but commercially grown in Maharashtra, Tamil Nadu and West Bengal.

## Description of Herb

Turmeric is a perennial herbaceous plant, grows up to 90 - 120 cm height.

**Primary tubers** are at the base of aerial stem and ellipsoidal, bearing many rhizomes.

**Rhizomes** are yellow to orange, aromatic, highly branched, cylindrical.

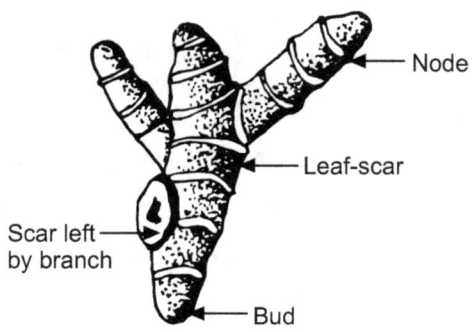

**Fig. 1.4 : Haridra rhizome**

**The leaves** are greenish yellow, with characteristic odor, ovate-lanceolate, with size of 25 - 40 × 10-15 cm. the apex of leaves are caudate- acuminate, base are narrow and tapering. The leaves are arranged as alternate. They are divided into leaf sheath, petiole and leaf blade.

**Flowers** pale yellow in long spikes of 10 - 15 cm. The bracts are light green and ovate with a length of 3 to 5 centimeters to oblong with a blunt upper end. Flowers during rainy season. Seeds are black and shining with large, lancerate and white aril.

## Macroscopic Characters

| | | |
|---|---|---|
| **Colour** | : | Outer colour of rhizomes is brownish yellow, Intenal colour varies from yellow to yellowish orange. |
| **Odour** | : | Characteristic aromatic. |
| **Taste** | : | Slightly bitter. |
| **Shape** | : | Round, cylindrical branched. |
| **Size** | : | 5 to 10 cm × 2 to 4 cm |

There are two types of Haldi :

(1)  Kapur Haldi,          (2)  Ran Haldi

## Cultivation and Collection

Turmeric can be grown in diverse tropical conditions from sea level to 1500 m above sea level, at a temperature range of 20-35°C with an annual rainfall of 1500 mm or more, under rain fed or irrigated conditions. it thrives best in well-drained sandy or clay loam soils with a pH range of 4.5 - 7.5 with good organic status.

The land is prepared as fine tilt with four deep pluging. Beds are prepared in after monsoon rain, beds of 10 m wide and 15 cm height are prepared with 50 cm between the beds. The propagation is carried out either of healthy and disease free whole or split mother and finger rhizomes. Rhizomes are planted in beds with decomposed cattle manure or compost at distance of 25 - 30 cm.

Farmyard manure (FYM) or compost @ 30 - 40 t/ha is applied by broadcasting and ploughed at the time of preparation of land gives best results. Biofertilizer (Azospirillum) and NPK is also recommended. Proper weeding has to be carried out.

The crop becomes ready for harvest in 7 - 9 months after planting during January - March. The land is ploughed and the rhizomes are gathered by hand picking or the clumps are carefully lifted with a spade. The harvested rhizomes are cleared of mud and other extraneous matter adhering to them. The fingers are separated from mother rhizomes. Mother rhizomes are usually kept as seed material.

## Preparation of Haldi

### Curing-drying and Polishing :

Fresh turmeric is cured for obtaining dry turmeric. Curing involves boiling of fresh rhizomes in water just enough to immerse them and drying in the sun. Artificial drying, using cross-flow hot air at a maximum temperature of 60°C.

Dried turmeric has a poor appearance and a rough dull outer surface with scales and root bits. The appearance is improved by smoothening and polishing the outer surface by manual or mechanical rubbing.

## Chemical Constituents

More than 100 components have been isolated from turmeric. In a standard form, turmeric contains moisture (> 9%), curcumin (5 - 6.6%), extraneous matter (< 0.5% by weight), mould (< 3%), and volatile oils (< 3.5%).

The main component of the root is a volatile oil, containing turmerone, and there are other coloring agents called curcuminoids in turmeric. Curcuminoids consist of curcumin demethoxycurcumin, 5'-methoxycurcumin, and dihydrocurcumin, which are found to be natural antioxidants.

**Turmerone**                **Curcumin**

The components responsible for the aroma of turmeric are turmerone, arturmerone, and zingiberene. The rhizomes are also reported to contain four new polysaccharides-ukonans along with stigmasterol, R-sitosterol, cholesterol, and 2-hydroxymethyl anthraquinone. Turmeric is also a good source of the w-3 fatty acid and a-linolenic acid (2.5%).

Nutritional analysis showed that 100 g of turmeric contains 390 kcal, 10 g total fat, 3 g saturated fat, 0 mg cholesterol, 0.2 g calcium, 0.26 g phosphorous, 10 mg sodium, 2500 mg potassium, 47.5 mg iron, 0.9 mg thiamine, 0.19 mg riboflavin, 4.8 mg niacin, 50 mg ascorbic acid, 69.9 g total carbohydrates, 21 g dietary fiber, 3 g sugars, and 8 g proteins.

## Standards of Quality

| | | |
|---|---|---|
| FOM | ⊁ | 2.0 percent |
| Total ash | ⊁ | 10.0 percent |
| Acid insoluble ash | ⊁ | 2.0 percent |
| LOD | ⊁ | 12.0 percent |
| ASE | ⊀ | 6.0 percent |
| WSE | ⊀ | 12.0 percent |

## Ayurvedic Properties

| | | |
|---|---|---|
| **Rasa** | : | Tikta, katu |
| **Guna** | : | Rooksha, Laghu, |
| **Veerya** | : | Ushna |
| **Vipak** | : | Katu |

## Pharmacological Uses

Aromatic, stimulant, tonic and carminative. Internally juice is anthelmintic. The petroleum ether extract and their two fractions showed significant anti-inflammatory activity in experimental rats. In another study, petroleum ether, alcoholic and aqueous extracts showed antifertility activity.

The volatile oil of rhizomes exhibited strong anti-inflammatory activity in experimentally induced edema and arthritis. In similar study the essentia oil and curcumin pigments are found as cholagogue. The preclinical animal study curcumin was found to cause sharp but transient fall of blood pressure. Along with anti-inflammatory activity of curcumin powder also posses gastro protective ability by increased secretion of mucin in gastro-intestinal linings.

## Therapeutic Uses

- The rhizomes are aromatic, stimulant, carmirative, alterative, blood purifier, antiperiodic and tonic. Externally, these are applied to sprains and on wounds. The fresh juice of its rhizomes is considered anthelmintic and is used as antiparastic in many skin affections and the rhizome decoction in purulent conjunctivitis.

- The essential oil obtained from its leaves also possesses antimicrobial activity against some bacteria. The smearing of turmeric paste on the face and limbs during bath clears the skin blemishes and beautifies the face and also checks the growth of hairs on skin. In pemphigus and shingles, the affected part first is smeared with a thick coating of mustard oil and dusted with turmeric powder. This cures the disease within 2 to 4 days. The smoke of turmeric powder gives relief from scorpion-stings. Besides, the fumes of its burning roots are also employed in hysteric fits.

- The decoction of fresh rhizome with coriander and cinnamon used for relief of catarrhal cough.

- The rhizome is recommended for intermittent fever, dropsy, jaundice, liver disorders, and urinary diseases.

- Turmeric alone or combined with die pulp of neem leaves is used in ringworms, obstinate itching, eczema and other parasitic skin diseases.

- In Ayurvedic and Unani practice it is used as a stomachic, tonic, blood purifier and alternative.

- Turmeric mixed milk is a household remedy and beneficial in the common cold."

## Traditional Uses

1. Paste of rhizomes is used externally on wounds as an antiseptic.
2. Turmeric paste alongwith neem paste is applied externally as anti-inflammatory.
3. In the treatment of haemorrhoids, it is applied externally as anti-inflammatory.
4. It is used as good skin toner and is used in face packs and also in cosmetic products.

## Doses

Infusion - 4 to 8 ml; powder - 1-4 g.

## Market Formulations

1. **Ashwagandha Ghruta :** (Shree Baidyanath Ayurved Bhawan Pvt. Ltd. Kolkata).
2. **Haridra Khanda :** (Nagarjuna Ayurvedic group. Kalayanthani PO. Thodupuzha. Kerala).
3. **Allergin Granules :** (Nagarjuna Ayurvedic group, Kalayanthani PO. Thodupuzha. Kerala).
4. **Vicco Turmeric Varnishing cream :** Vicco Laboratory, Near Tata Hospital, Bhoiwada, Mumbai - 4000 012.

# JATAMANSI

## Synonyms

**English:** Indian Spikenard, Nardus root, Mountain Nard, Muskroot.

## History

In India, it is used since 3,000 years traditionally. It is used at the time of religious functions, e.g. 'Havana Samagri and medicinally. It is called Jatamansi, because it resembles Jata or the tangled hairs of tapasvi.

## Biological Source

These are dried matured roots and rhizomes of herb *Nardostachys Jatamansi* DC. Belonging to family Valerianaceae.

## Geographical Source

It is a flowering plant grows upto 3000 to 5000 m of height in the Himalayas, Nepal, China and India. It is also commonly found in Garhwal, Kumaun, Uttarakhand and Sikkim.

## Description of Herb

It is an erect perennial herb of 10 - 70 cm in height.

**Leaves** are radical, elongated and spathulate. Its cauline leaves are sessile and oblong or sub-ovate. The bottom leaves are 15 - 20 × 2.5 cm in size.

**Flowers** are one, two or five in numbers that are pink to blue in colour in dense cymes. It flowers during August to September.

**Fruits** are one cm long with oval shape having sharp apex.

**Rhizomes** are short, thick, dark grey in colour, crowned with reddish brown tufted fibrous remains of the petioles of radical leaves, which gives a bearded appearance.

**Roots** are long solid fattening, dark brown in colour with acrid, bitter taste. It is having characteristic flavour.

## Cultivation and Collection

The various trials of cultivation of jatamnsi were carried out. The successful cultivation and harvesting was carried out with following conditions.

Commercial cultivation of jatamansi successfully carried out at lower altitude ranging between 1800-2200 m. it requires sandy loam acidic soil with high humus content. Seeds are sown in nursery bed during Nov. - Dec. in polyhouses. Vegetative propagation through splitting of roots was found most successful with higher production within short period than cultivation through seedlings.

After six to eight weeks of age seedlings are transplanted in the field. However, fibrous root formation takes place only after third year of growth when, plants are raised by seedlings. About 44,000 plants are planted in one acre of land.

In initial days, beds needed excessive watering/irrigation to decrease the mortality rate. Irrigation requirement will change in respect of different months like no irrigation is needed during monsoon period; while May - June and September-October watering must be done at every two days interval. Litter manure treatment instead of live stock manure gives better results. Proper weeding should be carried out during cultivation.

## Harvesting

The harvesting carried out after 3 years of plant age by uprooting method. Plants should be harvested just before senescence after maturation to achieve the higher quantity of active contents i.e. during the months of September at lower altitude while in the months of October at higher altitude. The harvested roots washed and dried in shade. It yie ds 12 - 13q/ha of roots

## Macroscopic Characters

| | | |
|---|---|---|
| Colour | : | Externally dark brown; internally - reddish brown |
| Odour | : | Strongly aromatic |
| Taste | : | Acrid, slightly bitter and aromatic |
| Size | : | 3 to 7 cm long and 0.5 to 1.5 cm in diameter |
| Shape | : | Cylindrical |
| Extra feature | : | Fracture – Brittle, rhizomes are covered with brown fibers forming a network which are skeletons of sheathing leaf bases |

**Fig. 1.5 : Jatamansi herb**

## Chemical Constituents

The roots of the plant contain 1.9 % essential oil. Beside that roots also contain sesquiterpenes and coumarins. Jatamansone or valeranone is the principal sesquiterpene. Other sesquiterpenes include nardostachone, dihydrojatamansin, jatamansinol, jatamansic acid, jatamansinone, jatamansinol, oroseolol, oroselone, seselin, valeranal. nardostachyin. An alkaloid actinidine has also been reported.

**Jatamansone**              **Nardostachone**

## Standards of Quality

| | | |
|---|---|---|
| FOM | ≯ | 5.0% |
| Ash | ≯ | 9.0% |
| Acid insoluble ash | ≯ | 5.0% |
| A.S.E. | ≮ | 2.0% |
| W.S.E. | ≮ | 5.0% |

## Ayurvedic Properties

| | |
|---|---|
| **Rasa (Taste)** | : Bitter, Astringent, Sweet |
| **Guna (Characteristics)** | : Light, Unctuous |
| **Virya (Potency)** | : Cool, Calm |
| **Vipaka (Post Digestive Effect)** | : Pungent |
| **Effects on Tridoshas (Humor)** | : Pacifies all the three doshas. |

## Pharmacological Uses

The rhizome shown to posses antioxidant hepatoprotective, cardio protective, hypolipidemic, anticancer, anticonvulsant, antidepressant, antiparkinson, neuroprotective and nootropic activity.

## Traditional Uses

Aromatic, antispasmodic, diuretic and carminative. It improves complexion.

Tonic to circulatory, nervous, digestive, respiratory and reproductive systems.

Useful in kidney stones, jaundice, removes blood impurities, hysteria and other nervous, convulsive ailments (nervousness, anxiety, dysmenorrhea, insomnia).

It helps to ease heart palpitations, headache, flatulence, epilepsy and convulsions. It can be used for bronchitis, asthma and considered as brain tonic traditionally.

## Therapeutic Uses

- As a tranquilizer, sedative and central nervous system depressant, Musk Root is used to treat stress and nervine disorders.
- It is also known to treat irregular heart palpitations and as a remedy for high blood pressure.

## Side Effects

- Special care is required while administering this medicine to patients with high blood pressure.
- Women with heavy periods should avoid this herb during periods. It may increase menstrual flow.
- On excess dose, it may cause vomiting, twitching abdominal pain and purgation.
- It is best to avoid during pregnancy and lactation period.
- It can be given to children only under medical supervision.

**Dosage :** Powder : 1 - 3 g in divided doses.

## Substitutes

The roots of *Nardostachys jatamansi* (commonly known as "Jatamansi") and S. *vaginatum* (Bhootkeshi) are often confused with each other. Due to the resemblance in between external morphological characters and characteristic odour. The roots of S. *vaginatum* are being used as a substitute for N. jatamansi in the Indian herbal drug market.

# LASUNA

### Synonyms

Garlic

### Biological Source

It consists of dried matured bulbs of plant *Allium sativum* family – Liliaceae.

### Geographical Source

It is cultivated in Central Asia, Southern Europe, USA and India. It is found in all states of India and is cultivated as a spice or condiment crop.

### Cultivation

The cultivation practice is similar to onion. The soil may be sandy, loam or clay, though Garlic flourishes best in a rich, moist. sandy soil. Soil should be sufficiently tilted. Fairly large size bulb is preferred for sowing, the bulbs are sown about 2 inches deep and about 6 inches apart, leaving about 30 cms between the rows. Garlic beds should be in a sunny spot. They must be kept thoroughly free from weeds and are planted early in the spring, in February or March. The bulbs should be ready for lifting in August, when the leaves will begin to wither. They may probably not be ready till nearly the middle of September.

### Description of Herb

*Allium sativum* is a hardy bulbous plant. It grows up to 1.0 m in height. The leaves are long, narrow and flat like grass.

The bulb is of a compound nature, consisting of numerous bulblets. known technically as 'cloves', grouped together between the membraneous scales and enclosed within a whitish skin, which holds them as in a sac.

The flowers are placed at the end of a stalk rising direct from the bulb and are whitish, grouped together in a globular head, or umbel, with an enclosing kind of leaf or spathae, and among them are small bulbils.

### Macroscopic Characters

The bulbs are composed of several cloves, enclosed in white skin, bulbs are sub-globular with 4-6 cm in diameter and composed of 8-20 cloves.

**Fig. 1.6 : Lasuna bulb and bulblets**

## Cloves

| | | |
|---|---|---|
| **Color** | : | White to pink |
| **Odour** | : | Characteristic |
| **Taste** | : | Hot pungent |
| **Size** | : | 2-3 cm × 0.5-0.8 cm |
| **Shape** | : | Convex, one end tapering while other is flat |
| **Extra feature** | : | When crushed produces persistent odour |

## Chemical Composition

Fresh or crushed garlic also affords the sulfur-containing compounds alliin, ajoene, diallyl polysulfides, vinyldithiins, S-allylcysteine, and enzymes, B vitamins, proteins, minerals, saponins and flavonoids.

**Allicin**                                   **Alliin**

The phytochemicals responsible for the sharp flavor of garlic are produced when the plant cells are damaged. The enzymes stored in cell vacuoles trigger the breakdown of several sulfur-containing compounds stored in the cell fluids and these are responsible for the sharp or hot taste and strong smell of garlic. Allicin has been found to be the compound most responsible for the "hot" sensation of raw garlic.

It is good source of essential minerals such as selenium, germanium, tellurium, copper, manganese and other trace minerals

## Standards of Quality

| | | |
|---|---|---|
| Foreign organic matter | ≯ | 2.0 percent |
| Total ash | ≯ | 5.0 percent |
| Acid insoluble ash | ≯ | 5.0 percent |
| LOD | ≯ | 65.0 percent |

## Ayurvedic Properties

| | | |
|---|---|---|
| **Rasa** | : | Pungent and sweet |
| **Veerya** | : | Heating |
| **Vipika** | : | Pungent |
| **Guna** | : | Heavy, unctuous, penetrating |

## Traditional Uses

- According to Ayurvedic texts garlic is a nourishing tonic for the whole body, age-sustainers, rejuvenator, aphrodisiac.

- It very good adaptogen, boosts up immune system and promotes strength.

- It is recommended in cardiac diseases and oedema.

- It is prescribed in chronic fevers, throat infections, cough, asthma and tumours.

- It is carminative and have ability to correct digestion, anorexia thus useful to cure constipation.

- It helps in the healing of fractures and wounds.

- It is mild laxative, useful in piles and intestinal infestation.

- It is a potent antiseptic, disinfectant and healing agent in a host of degenerative diseases.

- In a prescription of Charaka, dehusked and dried 160 g Lasuna (garlic) is boiled in four times of milk and four times of water till water is evaporated. Intake of this milk was prescribed in cardiac disorders, fevers, tumours, abscesses, oedema, sciatica, arthritis, neuralgia.

- According to Kaashyapa Samhita, the herb is one of the best fertility-promoting drugs. Ashtaanga Sangraha also mentioned similar uses along with as an aphrodisiac and rejuvenating agent.

## Pharmacological Uses

- Garlic is proven to be strong anti-hyperlipidemic and antihypertensive clinically and pre-clinically in experimental animals.

- Garlic demonstrated broad spectrum antimicrobial (almost all pathogenic microorganism) effective against *Helicobacter pylori* and *Mycobacterium tuberculi*.

- The garlic extracts in experimental animals are found to exhibit antioxidant potenital. It also posses cardio protective effects in hypertension, atherosclerosis. ischemic heart disease and hyperlipidaemia induced atherosclerosis.

- It also demonstrated antidiabetic, hepatoprotective, neuroprotective and nephroprotective activity in experimental animals.

- The different in-vitro and in-vivo studies revealed its cancer chemoprotective ability in colorectal cancer, prostate cancer, breast cancer, gastric cancer, oral cancer, hepatic cancer and leukaemia.

- Garlic posses strong immunopotential ability and increase in the individual life expectancy has led to a concurrent increase in age-related chronic diseases of the cardiovascular, brain and immune systems.

## Dose:

Paste 3-4 g

## Market Formulations

1. **Dabur Lasunadi Vati :** Dabur India Ltd., Kaushambi Ghaziabad – 201010 Uttar Pradesh.

2. **Lasunadi Ghrita :** VHCA Herbals, Near Honey Garden, G.T Road, Ghauranda Karnal, 132ll4, Haryana

3. **Vacalasunadi Taila :** Nagarjuna Ayurveda, Kalayanthani PO, Thodupuzha, 685 588, Kerala.

# MARICHA

## Synonyms

Black-pepper; Pepper.

## Biological Source

Black-pepper are the dried unripe fruits of climbing vine *Piper nigrum* belonging to family Piperaceae.

## Geographical Source

It is indigenous and cultivated in south India on large scale. Malaysia, Indonesia, Sri Lanka, Brazil. In India it is found in Tamil Nadu, Kerala, Andhra Pradesh, Karnatak and Assam.

## Description of Herb

It is perennial climbing vine. It is stout and partly shade loving. The creeper bears roots at internode, with the help of which the vine climbs.

## Leaves

Leaves are ovate, oblong about 12.5 to 20 cm long and 5 to 12 cm broad with 2 to 4 ribs.

## Flowers

Flowers are small, unisexual and bisexual in racemes.

## Fruits

Fruits are round berries in racemes, fleshy, drooping spikes which are green, turns red, orange during ripening and black on drying.

## Seeds

Seeds are rounded, with thin coating and hard inside. Two types of seeds are available in the market, the black and white.

**White :** It is prepared by soaking overnight black pepper in water, since than the outer coating is peeled off to get white pepper.

## Cultivation

It is perennial climber cultivated on large scale by sowing seeds or by propagating cuttings. The plant raised from cutting starts bearing from second year and survive upto 15 years and seed raised plant start fruiting after 7 - 8 years and survive upto 60 years.

## Collection

The spikes of fruits after full maturity are hand plucked and dried in sunlight for 8 - 10 days cleaned, graded and stored. Perfect drying to ensure the colour is very essential.

Decorticated fruits white in colour are also sold in the market at high prices and are preferred. They are stored in well filled, well closed containers away from sunlight and in cool place.

## Macroscopic Characters

| | | |
|---|---|---|
| **Colour** | : | The fruits are blackish brown or grayish black. |
| **Odour** | : | Aromatic and pungent |

| | | |
|---|---|---|
| **Taste** | : | Pungent |
| **Size:** | | Fruits are 3.5 – 6 mm in diameter. |
| **Shape** | : | Globular and coarsely reticulate wrinkled with remains of stigma at apex |

**Fig. 1.7 : Black pepper, fruiting twig and fruits**

## Chemical Constituents

Pepper contains an alkaloid piperine, volatile oil, pungent resin, piperidine and starch. The volatile oil mainly contains phellandrene and caryophyllene.

Piperine

**Black pepper oil** is slightly greenish in colour, and mainly contains β-caryophylline, and has following properties.

| | | |
|---|---|---|
| **Density** | : | 0.864 - 0.884, |
| **Optical rotation** | : | −1° to −23° |
| **Refractive index** | : | 1.479 - 1.488 |

Oil is used as aromatic and condiment in foods.

## Standards of Quality

| | | |
|---|---|---|
| F.O.M. | : | ≯ 2.0% |
| Total ash | : | ≯ 7.0% |
| Acid in ash | : | ≯ 2.0% |
| L.O.D. | : | ≯ 12.0% |
| W.S.E. | : | ≮ 6.0% |
| A.S.E. | : | ≮ 6.0% |

## Ayurvedic Properties

### Dried Fruit

| | | |
|---|---|---|
| **Rasa** | : | Katu |
| **Vipak** | : | Katu |
| **Veerya** | : | Ushna |
| **Guna** | : | Laghu, Teekshna |

### Fresh Unripe Fruits

| | | |
|---|---|---|
| **Rasa** | : | Madhur |
| **Vipak** | : | Madhur |
| **Veerya** | : | Natushna |
| **Doshaghnata** | : | Vataghna, Kaphaghna, Pittakar. |

## Traditional Uses

(a) Honey and pepper powder is administered in cough like condition.

(b) In cases of inflammatory pain pepper powder alongwith asafoeteda powder is applied on affected area (rheumatic pain).

(c) Paste of pepper is used as rubefacient and stimulant.

(d) In regular malarial fever, a paste with pepper powder tulsi extract and honey is administered.

(e) Ghee and pepper powder is used in voice crack.

## Pharmacological Use

Pepper is acrid, pungent, hot, carminative, externally it is used as rubefacient and stimulant to skin and resolvent. The fruits shows fungicidal activity.

## Dosage

0.5 to 1 gram

## Adultrants

Seeds of papaya are adulterated with black-pepper seeds.

## Substitutes

Following are the substitutes for black-pepper, fruits :

(a) *Piper attenuatum*

(b) *Piper brachystachyme*

(c) *Piper longum*

## Storage

Maricha fruits are stored in gunny-bags commercially, while the decorated fruits which are white in colour are stored in well filled well closed tin containers away from sunlight and in cool place.

## Market Formulations

1. **Maricadi Gutika :** Shree Baidyanath Ayurved Bhavan Pvt. Ltd., Kolkatta (W.B.).

2. **Divya Trikatu Churna :** Patanjali Ayurved Ltd., Haridwar, Uttarakhand.

## Ayurvedic Market Products

Marichidyatail, Marichidya gutika, Marichadyaghruta.

# NAGARMOTHA

*Cyperus rotundus* is thought to have originated in India and then spread from there during the past 2,000 years (it first appeared in a Chinese medicine book around 500 A.D.). The rhizome is used in Ayurvedic medicine, usually called musta, mustak, or mustaka and is mentioned in the ancient Charak Samhita.

## Synonyms

English - Cyperus Nut grass

## Biological Source

These are dried roots and rhizomes of plant known *Cyperus rotundus* Linn family Cyperaceae.

## Geographical Source

It is commonly available in hotter parts of India upto 1800 m altitude.

## Description of Herb

It is perennial shrub, attains a height of 15 to 60 cm, it has a thin dark green stem. Leaves are elongated and 0.45 to 0.9 cm wide are sharp. The flowers are present at racemes of 5 to 20 cm in length. The nodes on the stem are thick that bear 1 cm diameter, rhizomes are oval shaped. The plant flowers in summer and fruits in winter. It is very troublesome weed and difficult to eradicate.

## Macroscopic Characters

| | | |
|---|---|---|
| **Colour** | : | Rhizomes are aromatic white internally and brown externally. |
| **Odour** | : | Fragment and aromatic |
| **Taste** | : | Aromatic |
| **Size** | : | 0.8 to 2.5 cm |
| **Shape** | : | Ovoid, tunicate |
| **Leaves** | : | Longer than stem, narrowly linear, whitish green in colour |
| **Flower** | : | Simple or compound umbel, rays 2.5 cm bearing short spikes of 3 - 10 spreading red brown spikelets, 10 - 50 flowered. |
| **Nut** | : | Broadly oval, trigonous grayish black. |

**Fig. 1.8 : Nagarmotha herb (flowering)**

## Chemical Constituents

It mainly contains aromatic oil (0.5 - 0.9%), composed of terpenoids like α-cyperone, β-selinene, cyperene, patchoulenone, sugeonol, kobusone, isokobusone, and sesquiterpene, rotundone. The flavonoids, glycosides, tannins and sterols are also present in the drug.

**Cyperene**       **Sugeonol**

## Standards of Quality

| | | |
|---|---|---|
| Foreign organic matter | ⊁ | 2 percent |
| Total ash | ⊁ | 8 percent |
| Acid-insoluble ash | ⊁ | 4 percent |
| Alcohol soluble extractive | ⊀ | 5 percent |
| Water soluble extractive | ⊀ | 11 percent |
| Volatile oil | ⊀ | 1 percent |

## Ayurvedic Properties

| | | |
|---|---|---|
| Rasa | : | Katu, Tikta, Kasaya |
| Guna | : | Laghu, Ruksha |
| Veerya | : | Sheet |
| Vipaka | : | Katu |
| Karma | : | Sothahara, Dipana, Grahi, Krmighna, Pachana, Visaghna, Pittakaphahara, Sthoulyahara, Trsnanigrahana, Tvakadosahara, Jvaraghna |

## Pharmacological Uses

- Blood and circulatory system. It reduces blood and plasma viscosity and is anti-histaminic.
- Digestive system anti-diarrheal.
- CNS-Sedative, tranquilizer, benzodiazepine receptor antagonist, inhibits sodium potassium, AT Pase in brain.
- It is claimed to have anticancer, antoxidant, anti-inflammatory, analgesic, smooth muscle relaxant additives.

## Therapeutic Uses and Traditional Uses

- Paste of rhizomes is used in skin related ailments it helps in relieving the itching. It also improves eyesight and is used in eyes related ailments.
- Powder is used in mental diseases and diseases like psychosis and epilepsy. It improves digestive system removes worms from the gastro intestinal tract. It also curbs infection and helps in purifying blood. Nagarmotha helps in normalizing the menstrual disturbances and breast discomfort, it helps in improving the skin ailments and in maintaining the normal body temperature.
- It is used as stomachic, stimulant, carminative, emmenagogue, diuretic, hypotensive, analgesic, anti-inflammatory, anti-dysenteric, anti-rheumatic.

## Ayurvedic Formulations

Mustakadi kwath, Mushtadi churna, Mustakarisht

## Storage

Should be kept in wall closed well filled containers in cool place away from light.

## Market Formulations

1. **Cystone Syrup :** Himalaya Drug Company, Makali, Bangalore - 562123.
2. **Lactomom Granules :** Biocin Genetics & Pharma, Satellite, Ahmedabad - 380015.

# NIRGUNDI

The plant finds mention in the verses of the *Charaka Somhita* which is *unarguably* the most ancient and authoritative textbook of Indian Ayurveda.

## Biological Source

It consists of flowering tops and leaves of plant *Vitex negundo* L. family Verbenaceae. In traditional systems the seeds, bark and roots are also used to treat various aliments.

## Geographical Source

Throughout India in the warmer zones; ascending to 900 - 1500 m in the North Western Himalaya.

## Description of Herb

The plant grows all over India, in wastelands, up to 1500 meters elevation. A large shrub or rather small tree grows 2 - 4 meters in height, with quadrangular branches and thin grey bark.

## Leaves

The leaves petiolate, smooth, exstipulate, opposite, palmately compound with 5 - 7 leaflets with a typical pungent odour.

## Flowers

The flowers are in interrupted spikes and corolla is bluish purple in colour as two-lipped 6 - 9 mm long, lanceolate, flower spikes in panicles upto 30 cm long.

## Fruits

The fruits are ovoid or obovoid, four-seeded drupes, black when ripe with a persistent calyx.

## Cultivation

It is widely planted as a hedge plant in between the fields and usually not browsed by the cattle. It can be reproduced readily from shoot cuttings. It produces root suckers which can also be utilized as planting material. An easily grown plant, it prefers a light well-drained loamy soil in a warm sunny position sheltered from cold drying winds succeeds in poor dry soils. Plants tolerate temperatures down to about −10°C. The leaves and stems are strongly aromatic. The flowers have a most pronounced musk-like perfume.

## Macroscopic Characters

### Leaf

| | | |
|---|---|---|
| **Colour** | : | Greyish green |
| **Odour** | : | Agreeable and aromatic |
| **Taste** | : | Bitter |

Leaves are palmately compound, petiole 2.5 - 3.3 cm long; 3 - 5 foliate; the middle leaflet narrowly lanceolate, acute, entire or rarely crenate, middle leaflet 5 - 10 cm long and 1.6 - 3.2 cm broad, with 1 - 1.3 cm long petiolule, remaining two subsessile; in pentafoliate leaf inner three leaflets have petiolule and remaining two sub-sessile.

Fig. 1.9 : Nirgundi flowering herb

## Chemical Constituents

The chemical constituents are the monoterpenes agnuside, eurostoside, luteolin and aucubin. Vitex negundo also contains the flavonoids casticin, chryso-phenol and vitexin. Vitex contains Chrysophenol D. which is a substance with anti-histaminic properties and is muscle relaxant.

Ancubin

## Ayurvedic Property

| | | |
|---|---|---|
| **Rasa** | : | Katu (pungent), Tikta (bitter) |
| **Guna** | : | Laghu (Ruksha), Ruksha (dry) |
| **Virya** | : | Ushna (hot) |
| **Vipaka** | : | Katu (pungent) |
| **Doshakarma** | : | Kapha-Vata Shamaka |

## Traditional Uses

- *Vitex negundo* Linn. has been designated as an anthelmintic and is prescribed as a vermifuge in the exposition on the *Charaka Somhito*.

- Pillows stuffed with Vitex negundo. leaves are used to dispel catarrh, headache and smoke the leaves for relief.

- Crushed fresh leaf poultice is applied to cure headaches, neck gland sores, tubercular neck swellings and sinusitis.

- Essential oil of the leaves is also effective in treatment of venereal diseases and other syphilitic skin disorders.

- A leaf decoction with *pimpli* is used in catarrhal fever with heaviness of head and dull hearing.

- A tincture of the root-bark provides relief from irritability of bladder, rheumatism and in dysmenorrhea. *Anubhoga Vaidya Bhaga*, a compendium of cosmetic formulations, describes *Vitex negundo* leaves along with *Azadirachta indica, Eclipta alba, Sphaeranthus indicus* and *Carum copticum* in a notable rejuvenation treatment known as *Kayakalpa*.
- *Vitex negundo* Linn. is commonly known as *Nisinda* in Unani medicine. The seeds are administered internally with sugarcane vinegar for removal of swellings.
- In China, the fruit of *Vitex negundo* Linn. in the treatment of reddened, painful and puffy eyes, headache and arthritic joints.

## Therapeutic Uses

- The leaves roots and fruits are used as febrifuge, tonic, vermifuge.
- They are useful in dispersing swellings of the joints from acute rheumatism

## Leaves

- The juice of the leaves is used for removing foetid discharges and worms from ulcers, whilst oil prepared with the leaf juice is applied to sinuses and scrofulous sores.
- Extracts of the leaves have shown bactericidal and antitumor activity.
- Leaves are insect repellents. Extracts of the leaves have insecticidal activity.
- The fresh leaves are burnt with grass as a fumigant against mosquitoes.
- Decoction of leaves may improve eyesight.

## Stem

A decoction of the stems of *Vitex negundo* Linn. is used in the treatment of burns and scalds.

## Fruit

- The fruits are used in the treatment of angina, colds, coughs, rheumatic difficulties etc.
- The fresh berries are pounded to a pulp and used in the form of a tincture for the relief of paralysis, pains in the limbs, weakness etc.
- It reported good results on premenstrual water retention and as gaiactagogue without harmful side effects.

## Root

Root juice is said to increases the growth of hair.

## Pharmacological Uses

Scientifically in preclinical studies the plant found to posses anti- inflammatory, antinociceptive activity, CNS depressant activity, antioxidant, anticonvulsant, hepatoprotective, hypoglycemic, Immunomodultory and drug potentiating ability.

## Dosage

Leaf juice 15 - 20 ml per day; leaf powder - 3 to 6 grams per day.

## Market Formulations

1. **Nirgundi Ghana :** Chaitanya Pharmaceuticals Pvt. Ltd., Hirawadi Road, Panchavati, Nasik (MS).
2. **Suartho Tablets :** Nay Bhadra Healthcare, Bhandup (W) Mumbai - 400078.
3. **Arkartho Tablets :** Arkashala, Satara, Dist. Satara (MS).

# PIPALI

## Synonyms

Pipali, Pimpali.

## Biological Source

It consists of dried fruiting spikes of climbing vine *Piper longum* belonging to family Piperaceae.

## Geographical Source

It is cultivated in Cherapunji, Hills of Meghalaya. It is found in almost all parts of India, major parts are West Bengal, Bihar, Assam, East Nepal, Konkan to Kerala, Annamaliai district of Tamil Nadu. It is also found in Singapore, Sri Lanka, Indonesia, Malaysia and Nikobar Islands.

## Description of Herb

It is a shade loving, aromatic climber, trailing on ground or climbing with support.

| | | |
|---|---|---|
| **Leaves** | : | 5 to 8 cm long entire, ovate or oblonge 5 - 7 ribbed. |
| **Flowers** | : | Flowers are dioecious, small or minute, inflorescence a spike, male spike narrow, female spike circular. |
| **Fruits** | : | Fruits are ovoid, oblong cylindrical. Sunk in fleshy spike, full grown riped spikes are red in colour and after drying they turn blackish or ash coloured. |
| **Types** | : | Gajapippali, Sihali pippali, Vanpippali. |
| **Parts used** | : | Fruit, roots, stems. |

## Macroscopic Characters of Pippali

| | | |
|---|---|---|
| **Colour** | : | Pale brown to dark brown |
| **Odour** | : | Aromatic spicy |
| **Taste** | : | Flat and sweat |
| **Size** | : | 2 to 50 min. length and 0.4 to 0.5 cm in diameter |
| **Shape** | : | Circular and elongated cylindrical. |

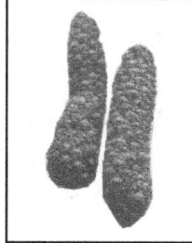

**Fig. 1.10 : Pipali fruits**

## Chemical Constituents

It consists of alkaloids piperine, piplertine, piplasterol, 1% essential oil and pungent resin.

**Piperine**

## Standards of Quality

| | | |
|---|---|---|
| F.O.M. | : | ≯ 2.0 percent |
| W.S.E | : | ≮ 10.0 percent |
| A.S.E. | : | ≮ 8.0 percent |
| Total ash | : | ≯ 8.0 percent |
| A. in ash | : | ≯ 3.0 percent |
| L.O.D. | : | ≯ 12.0 percent |

## Ayurvedic Properties

### Fresh (wet) spikes :

Rasa　　　　: 　Madhur;

Vipak　　　 : 　Madhur;

Veerya　　　: 　Shata Mukhya

Guna　　　　: 　Guru

### Dry Spices :

Rasa　　　　: 　Katu;

Vipak　　　 : 　Katu;

Veerya　　　: 　Anushna;

Guna　　　　: 　Laghu, Snigdha, Teekshna.

**Doshighnata :** Fresh (wet) : Kaphavat vardhak and pittashamak,

　　　　　　*dry* : Kaphaghana, Pittakar and Vaatshamak.

## Uses : Local :

Extract penetrates through skin and shows allergic reaction. It is used locally as anti-inflammatory and analgesic.

## Internal Uses :

## Digestive System

It is used as carminative, digestive, stomachic; very useful in conditions like enlarged spleen, good in cases of indigestion dyspepsia flatulent. Along with honey or ghee, it gives best results in hyperacidity.

## Circulatory Systems and Nervous System

Useful in anaemic conditions, in treating cases of tuberculosis. It is also used as brain tonic and in nervine disorders, like palsy gout, rheumatism and lumbago.

## Respiratory System

It is best used in respiratory tract infections in cases of acute asthma, bronchitis chronic, productive cough. It also shows antibacterial effect.

## Reproductive System

Useful in cases of dysmenmorhia, aphrodisiac, emmenagogne, in post partum - haemorrhage.

## Urinary System

It is used as diuretic.

## Dosage

Powder : 0.5 to 1 gram.

## Kalp

Gudpippali, pippalikhand, pippalyasari, chaushtapippali and sitopaledi churna.

## Storage

Preserve in well filled, well closed containers in cool place.

## Market Formulations

1. **Coliwell oil :** Lupin Laboratories Ltd. Bandra - Kurla Complex,Mumbai - 400051.
2. **Aurvel :** Oral Powder Meridian Enterprises Pvt. Ltd., Nariman Point - Mumbai 400001.

# SALLAKI

## Synonyms

Boswellia, Sallai-guggul, Indian Olibanum Tree.

## Biological Source

It is oleo gum resin consisting of exudate obtained from *Boswellia serrata* **Roxb.** Belonging to family Burseraceae.

## Geographical Source

About 10 species are available in tropical part of Asia and Africa, found in hilly areas of Madhya Pradesh, Bihar and Gujarat.

## Description of Herb

It is a moderate-sized highly branching deciduous tree with smooth, greenish or ash-coloured, papyraceous bark, growing upto 3 - 5 metre in height.

**Fig. 1.11 : Parts of sallaki tree**

- **Leaves** are alternate, imparipinnate and crowded towards the ends of branches; leaflets are 17 - 31 in number opposite, sessile, lanceolate or ovate, crenate and pubescent.
- Flowers are small and white, in axillary racemes or panicles.
- Drupes, the fruits are about 1.2 cm long and trigonous, splitting into 3 valves and subtended by the woody disk.
- Seeds are compressed and pendulous.

## Cultivation and Collection

*Bosewellia serrata* Roxb. is a species characteristic of the tropical dry deciduous forests. It is characteristically found on the slopes and ridges of hills, as well as on flat terrain, attaining a larger size on fertile soils. It is resistant to drought and resists fire better than other species in its zone of occurrence. The tree is also frost hardy and serves as a nurse tree for other species. In Maharashtra it is common throughout dry deciduous forests. It is collected from wild grown plants only.

Seeds have poor viability; They weigh 13,400 - 25,600 seeds/kg. Seeds are stored in dry tins, for not more than 6 - 9 months.

Natural regeneration is usually good, even in the poorest of locations. Some regeneration is done using coppice and suckers, but the species also reproduce fairly well from seed. Mature seeds may be collected from the trees to facilitate artificial propagation.

The seeds should be soaked in water before they are sown, to separate out the sterile pyrenes, which float on the surface. Seed germination takes between 7 and 15 days.

*Boswellia serrata* Roxb. has remarkable ability to survive and sprout from large branch or stem cuttings.

Flowering is during March - April and fruiting in winter season.

It is an exudates, which comes out from cortex after an injury or natural crack in the bark. It is fragrant, transparent, and golden yellow. After solidification, it turns into brownish yellow tears or drops and crusts. Its size varies from pea size to walnut size. The smell is agreeable.

Bark yields gum of quality after 8 years. The oleo-gum-resin is tapped by shaving off a thin band of bark about 20 cm wide and 30 cm long, at a height of 15 cm from the base of the tree. This initial blaze should be made to a depth of about half the thickness of the bark, viz. up to 0.75 cm. Tapping should start from November and stopped before the monsoon. The number of blazes required depends upon the girth of the tree. For continuous tapping on a 3-year cycle, the bole may be divided into three zones, each one being tapped for one year. The oleo-gum-resin is scrapped off and collected in a circular tray suitably placed around the trunk. It is collected in a semisolid state and the vegetable impurities are manually removed. It is then kept in baskets up to 30 days on a cemented and sloping floor, whence the fluid portion containing the volatile oil is collected and used in paints and varnishes. The remaining semi-solid to solid part is mainly gum - resin which is thoroughly dried and sometimes treated with soapstone powder to make it brittle. It is then broken into small pieces, cleaned and graded for marketing.

A mature tree yields about 1 - 1.5 kg of gum a year. It is said to be a good substitute for imported guggul. The gum collected by hand picking.

## Macroscopic Characters

| | | |
|---|---|---|
| **Color** | : | Transparent and golden yellow |
| **Odour** | : | Aromatic |
| **Taste** | : | Aromatic, bitter |
| **Size** | : | Varying |
| **Shape** | : | Irregular tears |

**Fig. 1.12 : Sallaki tears**

## Chemical Constituents

It is a oleo-gum-resin contains mixtures of essential oil, gum and resin. Its essential oil is a mixture of monoterpenes, diterpenes and sesquiterpenes. In addition phenolic compounds and a diterpene alcohol (serratol) is also found in essential oil. Gum portion of the drug consist of pentose and hexose sugars with some oxidizing and digestive enzymes. Resin is mainly composed of pentacyclic triterpene acid of which boswellic acid is the active moiety. The boswellic acid derivatives such as β-boswellic acid, acetyl β-boswellic acid and acetyl keto β-boswellic acid are confirmed, amongst β-boswellic acid is major. Recently new lupane triterpene and tetracyclic triterpene acids E, F, G and H from resin of bosewellia *serrata* have been reported.

**β-Boswellic acid**                                 **Serratol**

## Standards of Quality

| | | |
|---|---|---|
| FOM | ⊁ | 2.0 percent |
| Ash | ⊁ | 10.0 percent |
| Acid insoluble ash | ⊁ | 2.0 percent |
| Alcohol soluble extractives | ⊁ | 35.0 percent |
| Loss on drying | ⊁ | 12.0 percent |
| Melting point | : | 73 - 78°C |

## Ayurvedic Properties

| | | |
|---|---|---|
| Rasa | : | Tikta, madhur, Kashaya |
| Guna | : | Laghu, Ruksha |
| Virya | : | Sheeta |
| Vipaka | : | Katu |

## Traditional Uses

- Shallaki Boswellia *serrata*) is mentioned as a pain remedy in ancient Sanskrit texts dating back thousands of years. The herb is recommended in treating rheumatoid arthritis, osteoarthritis, gout, joint pain, skeletal muscle pain and back pain.
- Salai guggul is considered antiseptic, astringent. diaphoretic, diuretic, ecbolic, emmenagogue and expectorant. It is used beneficially in cutaneous and nervous diseases, cystic breast, chronic diarrhoea and dysentery, gout, goitre, piles, rheumatism, tumours and ulcers.
- Gum with acacia is used to correct foul breath. It effectively used as anti-obesity drug.

## Pharmacological Uses

- Boswellic acid has shown potential efficacy as anti-neoplastic agent in experimental primary and secondary brain tumors, in-vitro.
- Boswellic acid as exhibited strong antiarthritis potential by reducing the population of leucocytes, inhibit the migration of polymorphonuclear leukocytes in vitro and changed the electrophoretic pattern of synovial fluid protein in bovine serum albumin (BSA) induced arthritis.
- Sallaki also found to posses anti-inflammatory and anti-atherosclerotic properties by modulating p-glycoprotein, inhibiting the synthesis of 5-LOX products, topolsomerase, elastase and C-3 convertase enzymes, thus can be effective in the treatment of asthma, arthritis, cancer and ulcerative colitis.
- Alcoholic extract of Salai guggal in experimental studies demonstrated hepatoprotective, anti-asthmatic and anti-diabetic potential.
- Essential oil of oleo-gum-resin revealed stimulatory effect on skeletal muscles and spasmogenic effect on smooth muscle of guinea pig ileum.
- Acetyl-boswellic acid shows effectiveness in autoimmune encephalitis due to inhibition of ionophore stimulated release of leukotnienes from polymorpho-nuclear leukocytes.
- B. *serrata* was found effective in treating diarrhoea in patients with inflammatory bowel syndrome without causing constipation.

## Dosage

Sallaki 200 mg twice a day for 1st week, 200mg three times a day for 3 weeks.

## Market Formulation

1. **Sallaki capsule** : Himalaya drug company, Makali, Bangalore, Karnataka 562 162.
2. **Brihat jirakadi modak** : Sree Kundeswari Aushadhalya Ltd. Factory and P/O: Kundeswari. Bhaban Chittagong 4342, Bangladesh

# SUNTHI

## Synonyms

Zingiber, Zingiberis, Ginger.

## Biological Source

Sunthi consists of whole or cut, dried or fresh scrapped or unscrapped rhizomes of *Zingiber officinale* Roscoe, family Zingiberaceae. It contains not less than 0.8 per cent of total gingerols on dried basis.

## Geographical Source

It is said to be native of South East Asia, but is cultivated in Caribbean islands, Africa, Australia, Mauritius, Jamaica, Taiwan and India. More than 35 per cent of the world's production is from India.

## Cultivation and Collection

Approximately, 25,000 hectares of land is under cultivation in India for the production of about 25,000 tones of dry ginger annually. In almost all states of India, ginger is cultivated, especially in Kerala, Assam, Himachal Pradesh, Orissa, West Bengal and Karnataka. Ginger needs warm humid climate and is cultivated in areas with heavy rainfall. It is cultivated even at sea level, but still it thrives best at an altitude of 1000 - 1500 m. If no sufficient rainfall is available, proper arrangements for irrigation are necessary. Sandy or clay or red loamy soils are suitable for ginger. Ginger is cultivated by sowing rhizomes in the month of June. Carefully preserved seed-rhizomes are cut into small pieces and, at least one living bud is allowed in each piece. About 1200 - 1400 kg ginger seed-rhizomes are necessary per hectare. Ginger is a soil exhausting crop and being a rhizome, needs to be supplemented with good quantity of manures and fertilizers. Superphosphate, ammonium sulphate and potash are the common fertilizers used for ginger. Ginger is ready for harvesting in about six months, when its leaves become yellow. Harvesting of ginger is done by digging the rhizomes. They are washed properly and then dried to improve the colour and to prevent its further growth. The rhizomes are scrapped, dried and coated with inert material like calcium sulphate. The yield of 1500 kg per hectare of green ginger is possible by cultivation.

Sunthi is produced in almost all the states of India and ranks first among ginger producing countries of the world. There are one dozen large scale oleo resin producing industries in India at present with total installed capacity of 900 tones. 404.8 tones of spice oleo resins were exported during 1995 - 1996. Most of the exports are to US, UK, France, West Germany, Netherlands and Yugoslavia. Exports of ginger oil during 1994 - 95 and 1995-96 were worth ₹ 81.0 lakhs and 142 lakhs respectively.

## Macroscopic Characters

| | | |
|---|---|---|
| **Colour** | : | Externally, it is buff coloured. |
| **Odour** | : | Agreeable and aromatic. |
| **Taste** | : | Agreeable and pungent. |
| **Size** | : | Rhizomes of ginger are about 5 - 15 × 1.5 - 6.5 cm. |
| **Shape** | : | The rhizomes are laterally compressed, bearing short flat, ovate and oblique branches on the upper side, with bud at the apex. |
| **Fracture** | : | Short and fibrous. |

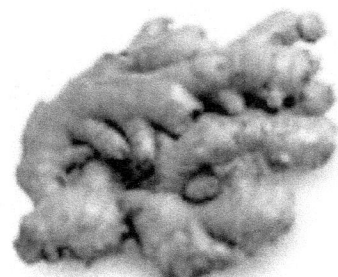

**Fig. 1.13 : Sunthi rhizome with buds**

Presence of nodes, internodes membranous scaly leaves and advantageous roots are the other character of rhizomes.

## Extra Features

Longitudinal striations and the occasional projecting fibres are present on the surface of ginger. Transversely cut surface shows well marked endodermis and stele.

## Chemical Constituents

Sunthi consists of volatile oil (1 - 4 per cent), starch (40 - 60 per cent), fat (10 per cent), fibre (5 per cent), inorganic material (6 per cent), residual moisture (10 per cent) and acrid resinous matter (5 - 8 per cent). Ginger oil is constituted of monoterpene hydrocarbons, sesquiterpene hydrocarbons, oxygenated mono and sesquiterpenes, and phenyl propanoids.

Sesquiterpene hydrocarbon content of all types of ginger oil from different countries is found to be same and includes α-zingiberene, β-bisabolene, α-farnesene, β-sesquiphellandrene and α-curcumene.

Aroma and flavour are the main characters of ginger. Aroma is due to fragrant principles of volatile oil while the flavour, pungency and pharmacological action is exerted by phenolic ketones of oleo-resin. Various components of volatile oil like isometric terpenic aldehydes like geranial and citral, which cause the delicate and lemony aroma. Few sesquiterpene oil hydrocarbons are believed to exert spicy note.

Phenolic ketones of oleo resin include gingerols like shogaols, zingerone, paradols, gingediols, hexahydrocurcumin and also o-methyl ethers of these compounds.

## Standards of Quality

| | | |
|---|---|---|
| FOM | - | not more than 2.0 per cent |
| Water soluble extractive | - | not less than 10 per cent |
| Alcohol (90 per cent) soluble extractive | - | not less than 45 percent |
| Total ash | - | not more than 6.0 per cent |
| Water soluble ash | - | not less than 1.7 per cent |
| Acid insoluble ash | - | not more than 2.0 per cent |

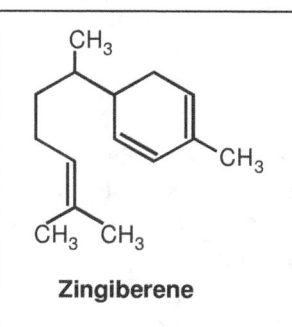

**Zingiberene**

## Ayurvedic Properties

| | | |
|---|---|---|
| **Rasa** | : | Katu |
| **Guna** | : | Snigdha, Teekshna |
| **Veerya** | : | Ushna |
| **Vipak** | : | Madhura∂ |

## Traditional Uses

Traditionally dry ginger is recommended for formulations.

Fresh ginger is pungent and hot and used for vomiting, cough, deliberating sweating and to reduce poisonous effects of other herbs. It is useful in nasal congestion, running nose, tooth ache, enhancing appetite, dyspepsia and intestinal infections. It should be used carefully in pregnancy.

## Uses

Sunthi is used as a stomachic, an aromatic, a carminative, stimulant and flavouring agent. Ginger oil is used in mouth washes, ginger beverages and liquors.

Sunthi powder has been reported to be effective in motion sickness. It has been suggested that adsorbent, aromatic and carminative properties of ginger on gastro-intestinal tract cause adsorption of toxins and acid enhanced gastric motility. These may have probably blocking effects of G. I. reactions and nausea.

*Zingiber officinale* (Methanolic extract) has molluscicidal effects, possessing efficacy to control the parasitic infection viz. schistosomiasis. U.S. Food and Drug administration has considers ginger as product that is generally regarded as safe (GRAS).

## Storage

Sunthi is coated with lime to improve its colour and quality and hence this particular variety is known as limed ginger.

## Adulterants

Sunthi is adulterated with exhausted ginger, but t can be detected by determination of water-soluble ash, volatile oil content and alcohol and water soluble extractives.

## Market Formulations

1. **Divya Trikatu Churna :** Patanjali, Ayurved Ltd., Haridwar, Uttarakhand 249401.
2. **Soubhagya Sunthi Pak :** Shri Baidyanath Ayurved Bhavan Pvt. Ltd., Kolkatta, West Bengal.

# TAMAL PATRA
## (Indian Bay Leaf)

There are different beliefs associated with the bay leaf. Some people belonging to the Elizabeth era believed that pinning bay leaves to one's pillow on the eve of Saint Valentine's Day can help them see their future spouse in their dreams.

## Synonyms

Tejpatta.

## Biological Source

It consists of dried leaves of plant *Cinnamomum tamala* belonging to family Lauraceae.

## Geographical Source

Uttarakhand, Darjeeling, Hills of West Bengal, Sikkim and Meghalaya.

## Cultivation and Collection

It is a small to moderately sized ever green tree. Plants are raised from seeds sown in nursery beds in March - April. Seedlings are transplanted to the field in rows of 2 m apart with a spacing of 3 - 3.5 m between plants. Leaves are collected in dry weather every year from vigorous plants, dried in the sun and tied up into bundles for marketing. Flowers are tiny, greenish yellow, insignificant. The plant produces flowers in last week of March or first week of April commonly pollinated by insects such as honey bees. After pollination it converts to drupe fruit and takes at least one year for maturity. Today, Indian bay-leaves are a spice used almost exclusively in the kitchens of Northern India, especially in the famous Moghul cuisine that was developed at the Imperial courts in Delhi and Agra.

## Description of Herb

It is a perennial or small evergreen tree, attaining 8 - 12 meters height and a girth of 150 cm.

* Stem rough with gray - brown, soft wrinkled bark which produces mucilage.

Fig. 1.14 : Tamal patra tree

The leaves are large, 12 - 20 cm long and 5 - 8 cm broad, ovate - lanceolate, thick leathery, acuminate, coriaceous, glabrous, shining green above and glaucous beneath, opposite, sub-opposite or alternate and short stalked; the midrib dividing some distance above the base into 3 longitudinal nerves, joined by distinct reticulate veins. Petiole slender, 0.8 - 1.8 cm long.

It has bisexual flowers, but on the same plant (monoecious). Flowers whitish, numerous, small, in axillary cymes and terminal pubescent panicles, pedicels are as long as calyx.

The fruit is an ellipsoidal drupe. Ripe fruits are dark purple in color and contain single seed.

## Macroscopic Characters

| | | |
|---|---|---|
| **Color** | : | Olive green |
| **Odour** | : | Strong cassia- or cinnamon-like aroma |
| **Taste** | : | Characteristics and spicy |
| **Size** | : | 10-15 cm in length, 3-5 cm in width |
| **Shape** | : | Ovate – lanceolate |
| **Extra feature** | : | Midrib dividing some distance above the base into 3 longitudinal nerves |

Fig. 1.15 : Tamal patra leaves

## Chemical Constituents

The major constituents of the leaf is essential oil these species contain furanosesquiterpenoids as principal constituents. Furanogermenone (59.5%) was found to be the major compound in the leaf essential oil is p-caryophyllene (6.6%), sabinene (4.8%), germacrene D (4.6%) and curcumenol (2.3%).

The leaf oil was characterized by presence of a-pinene, camphene, myrcene, limonene, eugenol, p-cymene, methyl eugenol, eugenol acetate and methyl ether of eugenol.

## Ayurvedic Properties

| | | |
|---|---|---|
| **Rasa** | : | Madhura, Katu |
| **Guna** | : | Laghu, Ruksha, tikshna |
| **Veerya** | : | Usna |
| **Vipaka** | : | Katu |

## Traditional Use

Used in anorexia, bladder disorders, dryness of mouth, nausea and spermatorrhea.

**Dose :** 1 to 3 gram.

## Pharmacological Uses

It has hypoglyacemic and hypolipidemic properties. It is also found to have good antioxidant, antimicrobial and antiulcer properties.

## Therapeutic Uses

- Ayurveda describes the use of leaves of tejoatra in the treatment of ailments such as anorexia, bladder disorders, dryness of mouth, coryza. diarrhea, nausea and spermatorhea.

- It is commonly used in many Ayurvedic preparations e.g. sudarshan choorna and chandraprabhavati.

- *Cinnamomum tamala* (tamalapatra) is one of the three ingredients of 'trijata' with *Cinnamomum zeylanicum* (tavak or dalchini) and *Elettaria cardamom* (elA), mentioned by Bhovaprakasa. Trijata is commonly used in Ayurvedic pharmacy in asava and arista preparation to augment the fragrance and to promote the appetite and digestion.

## Traditional Uses

It is used as appetizer, stomachic, mouth refresher, it is used to relieve colic (intestinal spasms) in joint pains, in the stress related conditions.

## Dose

1-3 g of the drug in powder form

## Market Formulations

| | | |
|---|---|---|
| 1. | **Bresal Syrup** | : Himalaya Drug Company. Makali, Bangalore 562123. |
| 2. | **Manix Capsule** | : Wockhard Limited, Bandra (East). Mumbai - 400051. |
| 1. | **Kasisadi Taila** | : Shree Baidyanath Ayurved Bhawan Pvt. Ltd. Kolkata, West Bengal. |
| 2. | **Chitrakadi Taila** | : Patanjali Ayurved Limited. Haridwar, Uttarakhand - 249401. |
| 3. | **Vajraka Taila** | : VHCA Herbals, Near Honey Garden, G.T Road, Gharaunda, Karnal - 132001, Haryana. |

# TULASI

## Synonyms

Surasa, Bhutaghni, Bahumangiri, Sulabha, Gramya, Swarasa.

## Biological Source

It consists of fresh or dried leaves, flowers and seeds of *Ocimum sanctum* belonging to family Lamiaceace.

## Geographical Source

It is found throughout India and in Himalayas upto 2000 mts. It is considered as sacred plant by Hindus.

## Cultivation and Collection

Commonly cultivated in gardens and also near temples. It is propagated by using seeds. Now-a-days cultivated commercially for its volatile oil (for Eugnol content) all aerial parts are collected after flowering.

## Description of Herb

Tulsi is a small much branched about 30 to 75 cm tall annual herb.

## Leaves

Leaves are tall to 2 cm ovate or oblong with entire a serrate margin softly hairy, with minute oil gland dots on dorsal side. Leaves, have aromatic flavour and slightly pungent taste.

## Flowers

Flowers are small in the from of elongated racemes about 12 to 14 cm long. They are purplish in colour with aromatic flavour.

## Fruits

Nutlets are subglobose, slightly compressed, pale brown or red in colour seeds are reddish-black and subglobose.

Seeds are reddish black and sub globose.

## Types

(a) **Shwet :** Leaves and branches are pale green in colour with flowers white in colour in raceme.

(b) **Krushna :** Dark green or blackish green in colour with purple flowers.

(c) **Ram Tulas :** Karpur tulas with camphor odour with long and matured inflorescence and leaves are bigger in size.

## Macroscopic Characters :

| | | |
|---|---|---|
| Colour | : | The leaves are green in colour and pubescent on both sides. |
| Odour | : | Aromatic and slightly pungent. |
| Taste | : | Aromatic and slightly pungent. |
| Size | : | 2.0 to 3.0 in length and 1 - 2 cm in width. |
| Shape | : | Oblong with acute apex and entire or serrate margin. |

**Fig. 1.16 : Twig of Tulsi herb**

## Chemical Constituents

Leaves of tulsi contain pleasant volatile oil, oil contains 70% eugenol, carvacrol, and eugenol-methyl-ether. It also contains caryophyllin, seeds contain high % of mucilage and fixed oil. The plant also contains alkaloids, glycosides, saponin, tannins, vitamin C and traces of maleic, citric and tartaric acid.

Eugenol                     Methyl eugenol

## Standards of Quality

| | | |
|---|---|---|
| Total ash | : | ⊁ 16.0 percent |
| Acid insoluble ash | : | ⊁ 6.0 percent |
| A.S.E | : | ⊀ 20 percent |
| W.S.E. | : | ⊀ 10.0 percent |
| Volatile oil | : | ⊀ 0.4 percent |

## Ayurvedic Properties

| | | |
|---|---|---|
| **Rasa** | : | Katu, Tikta |
| **Vipak** | : | Katu |
| **Veerya** | : | Ushna |
| **Guna** | : | Laghu, Snighda, Tikshna |
| **Seeds (Beeja)** | : | Snighda, Pichial. |

Leaves and inflorescence : Snigdha.

**Doshaghnata :** Kaphaghana, Vataghana and Pittaprakopak.

## Traditional Uses

(a)  Infusion of tulsi leaves is used in cases of chronic fever.

(b)  In malarial fever tulsi extract along with black pepper is useful.

(c)  Syrup of seeds is used as diuretic also as aphrodisiac.

(d)  In cases of amoebic dysentery infusion of seeds in morning is useful.

(e)  Leaf extract along with honey is useful in cases of cough (asthematic cases).

(f)  Leaf extract is used as antitoxide in scorpion bite extract is applied.

## Market Formulations

1.  **Tulsi Himalaya Syrup :** Himalaya Drug Co., Makali, Bangalore - 462123.

2.  **Honitus Syrup :** Dabur Pharmaceuticals Ltd., Caziyabad - 201010.

# VACHA

## Synonyms

English - Sweet flag.

## Biological Source

It consists of dried rhizomes of *Acorus calamus* Linn. belonging to family Araceae.

## Geographical Source

Vacha is a semi-aquatic perennial plant, commonly found in damp and marshy places in India. It is common found in Manipur and the Naga hills; also growing wild, ascending 2000 to 2000 metres in the Himalayan ranges.

## Description of Herb

A perennial, aromatic herb with creeping rhizomes.

- The **leaves** are yellowish green, 2-3 ft long, slender, sword -shaped and simple, arranged in two rows arising alternately from the horizontal rhizomes.

- **Rhizomes** are longitudinally fissured with nodes, somewhat vertically compressed and spongy internally.

- **Flowers** small disc shaped, fragrant, pale green in a spadix, bloom in the month of June.

- **Fruits** are a three-celled fleshy capsule with full of mucus. After maturity fall on ground.

- The **root** is about 1 cm thick, spreads within the soil and has distinct nodes and internodes. Numerous root fibres arise all over the internodes.

## Cultivation and Collection

The plant grows well in sandy-loam soils of wet and marshy places. Field should be ploughed thoroughly and farmyard manure should be added to it. It is propagated through division of rhizomes. Cutting of old rhizomes of 5-7 cm length are planted in poly-bags or directly in field in the month of July-August. The plant population should be maintained at the spacing of 30 × 30cm. Irrigate the field immediately after transplanting. Twice a week irrigation is required during dry and hot months.

Mature rhizomes are collected after 2-3 years of plantation, leaving daughter rhizomes for subsequent regeneration.

## Macroscopic Characteristics

Rhizomes used as peeled and unpeeled

| | | |
|---|---|---|
| **Colour** | : | Reddish grey |
| **Odour** | : | Pleasant aromatic |
| **Taste** | : | Pungent, bitter |

**Extra feature**    :    Shows node and internode, lower surfaces shows fibrous roots. It has fibrous fracture.

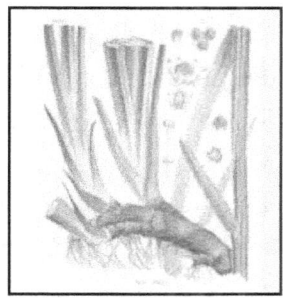

**Fig. 1.17 : Vacha herb with rhizome and root fibres**

## Chemical Constituents

The dried rhizomes contain 1.5 - 3.5 % of volatile oil. including p-Asarone (isoasarone) is usually the major terpenoid constituent. It also shows the other terpenoids a-Asarone, acorone, acorenone, acoragermacrone, calamusenone and elemicine. The other constituents includes cis-isoelemicine, cis and trans isoeugenol and their methyl ethers, camphene, p-cymene, p-gurjunene, a-selinene, p-cadinene, camphor, are also present.

$\alpha$-**asarone**                    $\beta$-**asarone**

## Standards of Quality

| FOM | ⊁ | 1.0 percent |
| Total ash | ⊁ | 6.0 percent |
| Acid insoluble ash | ⊁ | 0.5 percent |
| Alcohol soluble extractives | ⊁ | 20.0 percent |

## Ayurvedic Properties

| Rasa | : | Tikta, Katu |
| Guna | : | Lagu, Tikshna, Sar |
| Veerya | : | Ushna |
| Vipak | : | Katu |
| Prabhava | : | Medhya |

## Pharmacological Uses

1. The rhizome is an aromatic, stimulant, bitter, tonic. Carminative, antispasmodic, expectorant, emetic, emmenagogue, aphrodisiac, laxative, and diuretic.

2. The alcoholic extract of the plant has been shown to possess sedative and analgesic property; it causes a moderate depression in the blood pressure and respiration.

3. The volatile oil showed marked insecticidal activity due to presence of trans- isomer of asarone.

4. The water-insoluble fraction of the dealcoholized extract exhibited intestinal smooth muscle relaxant and negative inotropic action on frog's heart.

## Traditional Uses

1. It has capacity to digest the toxins and also removes the accumulated doshas from dhatus.

2. It is used to awaken digestive fire.

3. It is used as anthelmintic

4. It gives benefit in emotional problems and restores the consciousness.

5. It has ability to rejuvenate the mind.

6. It is also used to treat epilepsy.

7. Vacha powder is administered orally with honey and jaggery in dyspepsia.

8. In case of swellings, the paste of Vacha and mustard (Sarshapa) may be applied externally.

9. In treatment of migraine fine powder of vacha along with long pepper inhaled through nostrils.

10. It clears the throat and relives dry throat and cough. It increases the secretion of mucous membrane and salivary glands.

11. Juice of rhizome applied externally in treatment of boils. It is also applied in arthritic and rheumatic conditions as an anti-inflammatory agent.

12. Juice of rhizomes widely used in teething problems of children.

## Dose

Dried powder - 125 - 500mg per day for therapeutic use.

## Market Formulations

1. **Brahmi ghrita** : Brahmi, Bach, Kut, Shankhpushpi and ghrit Shree Baidyanath Ayurved Bhawan Pvt. Ltd. Kolkata.

2. **Saraswat Churna** : Vacha, Shankhpushpi, Aswagandha, Bramhi, etc. Shree Baidyanath Ayurved Bhawan Pvt. Ltd. Kolkata.

3. **Divya Sanjeevani Vati** : Patanjali Ayurved Limited, Haridwar, Uttarakhand – 249401.

4. **Vachalasunadi Enna** : *Acoras calamus (vacha), Curcuma longa (haridra), Aegle marmelos (bilwa);* Asoka Pharmaceuticals, Asoka Building, Main Road, Kannur, Kerala - 670 001.

# VIDANGA

Vidanga is one of the powerful anti-parasitic herbs of Ayurveda. It is widely used against intestinal worm infestation. Its botanical name is *Embelia ribes*. It is called **False black pepper**, because it mimics pepper in appearance.

## Synonyms

Embelia.

## Biological Source

It consists of berries of plant *Emberlia ribes burn f.* belonging to family Myrsinaceae; In traditional medicine the barks and leaves are also recommended in treatment of diseases.

## Geographical Source

It grows in semi evergreen and deciduous forests at an a titude of 1,500 m, throughout India. Naturally found in the Western Ghats, Tamil Nadu and Karnataka states of India.

## Description of Herb

A large scandant straggling shrub with a long slender brittle stem. It is a Climbing creeper shurb, flexible, and terete branches:

- Bark studded with lenticels.
- Leaves are simple, elliptic, lanceolate, 6-14 cm long and 2-4 cm wide and entirely glabrous, short and obtusely acuminate. They are alternate in arrangement.

  Flowers small, greenish yellow to whitish yellow colored.
- Fruits about the size of white pepper, reddish brown to blackish berry, 2-2.4 mm smooth. The outer covering of the fruit is fragile and inside the seed is spotted.

**Fig. 1.18 : Vidanga fruiting herb**

## Cultivation and Collection

The plant can be grown in variety of soils including light black cotton soil, sandy/rocky in different agroclimatic conditions in tropical regions up to 800-1500m. altitude. The seeds 5 kg/hector) are sown in well prepared nursery beds in May - June. The seedlings of six months are transplanted in to the heavily manured field at a distance of 60 × 60 cm. The seedlings can also be planted in pits of 1 × 1 feet size. Compost/Vermi compost, organic manure is preferred. Proper weeding and thinning should be performed whenever required. Plants are semi irrigated may require once in 15 days irrigation.

Usually fruiting starts in August-September after 2 years of plantation and fruit ripes during November to January. The fruits are collected manually, dried in shade, and stored in clean porous Jute-bags. The plant is allowed to grow further.

## Ayurvedic Properties

**Vidang** Kul has the following Ayurvedic Properties:

| | | |
|---|---|---|
| **Rasa (Taste)** | : | Kashaya (Astringent), Katu (Pungent) |
| **Guna (Properties)** | : | Laghu (Light), Tikshan (Sharp), Ruksha (Dry) |
| **Veerya (Potency)** | : | Ushan (Hot) |
| **Prabhav (Effect)** | : | Wormicide |

## Macroscopic Characters

The fruit is globular and wrinkled, varying in colour from dull red to nearly black.

## Fruits

| | | |
|---|---|---|
| **Color** | : | Blackish brown |
| **Odour** | : | Distinct |
| **Taste** | : | Astringent |
| **Size** | : | 2.4 - 4 mm |
| **Shape** | : | Sub globular |
| **Texture** | : | Wrinkled |

**Extra feature:** Fruit bears a short pedicel with brittle pericarp enclosing a single seed covered with a membrane.

**Fig. 1.19 : Vidang berries**

## Chemical Constituents

The main active constituents are - Embelin, Embeliaribyl ester, Embelinol, Embeliol, Potassium embelate.

Plant also found to contain other constituents like an alkaloid christembine, a resinoid, tannins and minute quantities of a volatile oil, quercitol and fatty ingredients.

**Embelin**         **Vilangin**

## Standards of Quality

| | |
|---|---|
| Total ash | ≯ 5.0% |
| Acid insoluble ash | ≯ 1.0% |
| Alcohol soluble extractive | ≮ 3.0% |
| W.S.E. | ≮ 7.0% |

## Traditional Uses

- Appetizer; Mild Laxative; Carminative; Anthelmintic.
- It is believed to be useful in snake bite (resists poison), but it is not sufficient antidote to the venom.
- Useful against skin diseases, bronchitis, urinary discharges, dyspepsia, liver ailments, jaundice, hemicrania, worms in wounds etc. among others.
- It is a common practice to put a few berries of the plant in the milk that is given to young children as it is believed to prevent flatulence.
- Sushruta describes the fruit as anthelmintic, alterative and tonic, and recommends their use along with liquorice root, for the purpose of strengthening the body and preventing the effects of age.
- It is used in 75 ayurvedic preparations.

## Therapeutic Uses

### Roots

- Embelia root bark is acrid, astringent, anthelmintic, carminative, digestive, laxative, soothing, stimulant, stomachic, and thermogenic.
- It is used in treating fungal infections of skin and mouth ulcers,

- Roots are also useful in headache, toothache and sore throat, hemorrhoids, obesity, piles, Its decoction is useful in insanity and heart diseases.

- Is used in antifertility, antioestrogenic, and in lung diseases and pneumonia,

- The root decoction is taken for treating insanity and heart diseases.

- It is very effective anthelmintic medicament.

## Leaves

- Leaves possess astringent, thermogenic, demulcent and depurative properties. They are useful in skin diseases and leprosy.

## Fruits

- Embelia fruits are acrid, bitter, astringent, febrifuge, stimulant, anthelmintic and useful in fever.

- Fruits also used as carminative, dyspepsia, flatulence, colic, diuretic and laxative.

- They are useful in leprosy, nervous debility, tumors, asthma and general debility

- The fruit paste is used as a mouth wash to combat cavities, and also applied externally for skin related problems.

## Pharmacological Uses

- Alcoholic extract of berries exhibited antioxidant, antifertility activity, anti-androgenic and anti-oestrogenic activity in preclinical studies.

- Methanol and aqueous extract of E. ribes showed moderate activity against multi-drug resistant *Salmonella typhi*.

- Embelin and their derivates showed analgesic, antibacterial, antifertility and wound healing activity; further more it exhibited chemopreventive effect against DENA/PB-induced hepatocarcinogenesis in Wistar rats.

- In experimental studies; aqueous extracts of E. ribes showed antidiabetic and antihypertensive potential.

## Dosage

Powder 3-5 g per day, in divided dose.

## Market Formulations

1. **Avipattikar Churna :** Shree Baidyanath Ayurved Bhawan Pvt. Ltd. Kolkata.

2. **Medohar Vidangadi Loha :** Unjha Ayurvedic Pharmacy, Dhanwantary Prasad, Station Road, Unjha - 384170, Gujarat.

3. **Vidangarishta :** Sandu Pharmaceuticals Ltd. Sandu Nagar, D. K. Sandu Marg, Chembur, Mumbai, Pin: 400 071, Maharashtra.

# MUSK

## Synonyms

Moschus, Kasturi.

## Biological Source

Musk is a dried secretion obtained from the prenaptial follicles of male musk-deer *Moschus moschiferus* Linn family Cervidae.

## Geographical Source

The animal musk-deer (Fig.) is found in the mountainous regions of the Himalayas and in China. It is also reported in Russia.

## Processing of Musk

Musk deer is a small animal of 50 cm height and differs from other deers in respect that they have long ears and fangs, there are no antlers in either sex. It is a wary animal of iron-grey colour.

**Fig. 1.20 : Musk-deer**

The musk is contained in an oval hairy projecting sac found only in the male, situated between the umbilicus and the prepuce. The sac, also known as pod, is about 3 - 7 cm long and 3 - 5 cm broad. It weighs about 30 g and contains half its weight of musk. The sac opens by a small hairy orifice on its anterior part and marked posterior by a groove or furrow, which corresponds with the opening of the prepuce.

## Description

| | | |
|---|---|---|
| **Colour** | : | Dark brown or brownish-red mass |
| **Odour** | : | Very strong and diffusible for long t me |
| **Taste** | : | Slightly bitter and aromatic |

Musk occurs as viscid mass or coarse granular powder, slightly unctuous.

## Extra Features

Aqueous solution is faintly acidic, It stains paper pale yellow, when burnt gives off urineous smell. Smell of Kasturi, totally disappears when tritrated with camphor, bitter almonds, garlic or oily seeds. Evey thing in its vicinity retains the flavour for long time.

## Chemical Constituents

When distilled, musk yields about 1.5 per cent w/w of dark brown volatile oil. It also contains, fat, wax, cholesterin, albuminoids and resins.

The volatile oil chiefly contains ketonic substances, of which muskone is the main constituent.

## Standards of Quality

| | | |
|---|---|---|
| **Loss on drying** | : | 20 - 30 per cent |
| **Alcohol soluble extractive** | : | 20 - 30 per cent |
| **Water soluble extractive** | : | 55 - 70 per cent |
| **Total Ash** | : | 08. - 0 per cent |

## Uses

It retains its odour for very long time and the smell is perceptible even if diluted to 3000 times. Due to this property, it is used in perfumery. It is used as flavouring agent for cosmetic product and also for toilet soaps. Therapeutically, it is administered as powerful stimulant in the treatment of hysteria.

## Traditional Uses

Used as flavouring agent for cosmetic products.

## Substitutes

There are several animals that secrete substances with strong odour, more or less similar to musk. Beaver (*Castor fiber*), civet (*Viuerra zibetha*) and American musk (*Fiber zibeythicus*) are few important examples.

The herbal source, known as Musk mallow (*Abelmoschus moschatus*, family *Malvaceae*) is found abundant in hotter plains of India. This plant is cultivated in Maharashtra, Gujarat, and M.P. The seeds of this plant contain volatile oil, which has resembling flavour to that of musk.

Synthetic musk is a yellowish white crystalline compound and has very strong persistent odour, somewhat similar to, but distinct from natural musk.

## Storage

It should be stored in well closed containers in cool place away from sunlight.

✍ ✍ ✍

# Chapter 2

# LIPIDS

## BHILAMA

### Synonym

Marking nut, Bibba.

### Biological Source

This consists of fully matured dried fruits of the plant known as *Semicarpus anacardium,* family Anacardiaceae.

### Geographical Source

Plant occurs on wild in the sub-Himalayan tract upto 1000 metres in Assam, Khasi hills, Madhya Pradesh, Gujarat, Konkan (Maharashtra) and decidous forests of South India.

### Description of Herb

It is deciduous tree of sub Himalayan tract ascending upto 1200 meters.

### Macroscopic Characters

Similar to cashew nut it has orange fleshy false fruits, which are edible.

True fruits of marking nut has

| | | |
|---|---|---|
| **Colour** | : | Black or dark brownish black with glossy appearance |
| **Odour** | : | Characteristic |
| **Taste** | : | Bitter and acrid |
| **Size** | : | 1.5 – 2 cm |

Juice of the fruit is highly vesicant, fruits are used to mark the clothes by washerman (marking nut).

Kernels known as **Godambi** are edible and used alongwith dry fruits. Fruits are somewhat triangular thick and oily.

**Fig. 2.1 : Marking nuts**

( 2.1 )

## Chemical Constituents

Bark of the marking nut contains gum resin, while the fruits and kernels contain fixed oil.

Pericarp contains about 32.0 percent of fixed oil which is vescicating while kernels contain sweet and edible fixed oil.

Pericarp juice contains anacardic acid, and cordial monohydroxy phenol named as semicarpol (b.p. 185 – 190°C), dihydroxy compound known as bhilawanol (b.p. 225 – 226°C) about 18.0% and 15.0%, non-volatile corrosive residue and traces of volatile oil.

$$(CH_2)_7 . CH : CH (CH_2)_5.OH$$

Bhilawanol

## Ayurvedic Properties

| | | |
|---|---|---|
| **Rasa** | : | Madhur |
| **Guna** | : | Snigdha, Tikshna |
| **Veerya** | : | Ushna |
| **Vipak** | : | Madhura |

## Uses

Marking nut tree exudes gum resin which is used in leprosy, syphilis, veneral infections and nervous debility.

Juice from the nut is used as an anti-inflammatory in rheumatism asthma, epilepsy, psoriasis, warts and also for timorous.

## Dose

1 to 1 drops (Juice).

## Traditional Use

Traditionally the fruit oil when mixed with coconut or seasame oil is effectively used to prevent pus formation and also as a powerful analgesic.

## Caution

Fruits being vesicant should be handled very carefully.

# CASTOR OIL

Due to violent action castor seeds are never used internally. However, they are used as source of castor oil.

## Biological Source

Castor oil is the fixed oil obtained by the cold expression of the kernels of seeds of *Ricinus communis*. Family *Euphorbiaceae*.

## Geographical Source

Castor seeds are produced in almost all tropical and sub-tropical countries. In India, castor is one of the major oil seed crops and India is the second largest producer of castor seeds in the world, producing about 2.8 lakhs tonnes per annum. Brazil, U.S.S.R. Thailand, U.S.A., and Rummnia are other countries producing drug on large scale. In India, it is largely grown in Andhra Pradesh, Gujarat and Karnataka. Andhra Pradesh is producing about 60 % of the total crop in India.

## Preparation of Castor Oil

Castor seeds are rich in phosphorous contents and most of it is in the sphytin. Hull is rich in mineral and also contains an alkaloid ricinine, resir, pigment etc. The oil content of the kernel varies from 36 to 60 %. Amongst different varieties, Hyderabad muggelai variety is supposed to be the richest (about 48 %) in oil content.

Castor oil can be prepared by two different methods : the first being the crushing of whole or decorticated seeds in power driven hydraulic presses and the second one known as Ghani, which consists of manually operated screw press driven by bullocks. For commercial scale of extraction, the first method is adopted. The oil, thus produced, is a non-medicinal castor oil.

First of all, the seeds are graded and made free of impurities like metallic pieces of iron and sand. The seeds are decorticated and hulls are removed. If the seeds are not decorticated, the manurial value of the cake increases. But for medicinal purposes, it is' desired that the seeds should be decorticated, as it improves colour of the oil and also helps in controlling acid value of oil.

Decorticated seeds are pressed under the hydraulic press with a pressure of 2 tonnes per square inch, which helps in extracting out 30 % of the oil present in the seeds at room temperature. The oil is known as cold drawn oil. Rest of the oi from the seeds is removed by further increasing pressure, and sometimes by hot pressing cr even by solvent extraction process. The oil, thus processed, is not suitable for medicinal purposes. The co d drawn oil is then steamed at 80°C, to destroy the enzyme lipase and ricin (toxic protein). It is then bleached and deacidified with sodium carbonate to remove free fatty acid. If necessary, oil is washed with hot water before steaming to remove mucilaginous matter present in oil. Finally, it is treated with activated earth or animal charcoal to remove final impurities by adsorption and f lled 0 into the containers.

## Organoleptic Characters

**Colour**      :     Pale yellow or almost colourless liquid.

**Odour**       :     Nauseating.

**Taste**       :     First it is bland, but afterward slightly acrid, and usually nauseating.

It is viscous and transparent liquid.

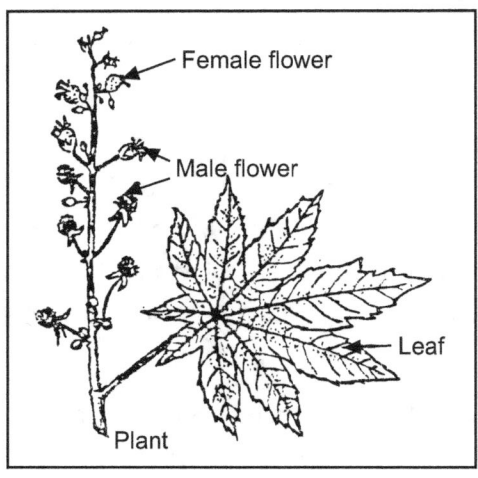

**Fig. 2.3 : Castor Plant (Flowering)**

## Solubility

It is soluble in alcohol, (an exception to the category of fixed oils), miscible in chloroform, solvent ether, glacial acetic acid and petroleum ether.

## Chemical Constituents

Castor oil chiefly contains triglyceride of ricinoleic acid (about 80 %) Other glycerides are also the other present in the drug, the fatty acids represented are isoricinoleic, linoleic, stearic and isostearic acids. The viscosity of the castor oil is due to ricinoleic acid.

Ricinoleic acid : $CH_3(CH_2)5CHOH\ CH_2\ CH = CH\ (CH_2)_7\ COOH$

## Standards of Quality

1. **Weight per ml**    :    0.945 to 0.965

2. **Acid value**        :    Not more than 2

3. **Acetyl value**      :    Not less than 143

4. **Iodine value**      :    82 to 90

5. **Sap value**         :    177 to 185

6. **Optical rotation**    :    Not less than + 3.5°

## Identification

1. It mixes with half its volume of light petroleum ether (40 - 60°) and is partly soluble in its two volumes.

2. Add to the oil an equal volume of alcohol; clear liquid is obtained. On cooling at 0°C and on storage for three hours; the liquid remains clear.

## Ayurvedic Properties

Rasa     :  Madhur katu

Guna     :  Snigdha

Veerya   :  Madhur

Vipak    :  Ushna

## Uses

Castor oil is used as a cathartic. It is also used for lubrication commercially. Several other forms of the castor oil like dehydrogenated castor oil (DCO) and hydrogenated castor oil (HC) are used industrially for several other purposes. The fatty acids like ricinoleic; heptaldehyde and undecenoic acid are the other substances commercially prepared out of castor oil.

The cathartic property of castor oil is due to irritant action of ricinoleic acid. Castor oil is often given orally or as aromatic castor oil or in the form of capsules. It is used in abortificient paste and ricinolic acid is used in contraceptive creams and jellies. Atropine and cocaine for opthalmic purposes are suspended in castor oil. As an emollient it is used in preparation of lip-stick and as sulphorecinolate in tooth formulation being strong bactericide. Other cosmetic purpose for which the oil is used includes perfumed hair oil and hair fixers.

Turkey red oil and soap are other commercial products, extensively used in textile industry. The castor oil is used in the preparation of paints, enamel, varnishes, grease, polishes, printing ink, hydraulic and brake spirit with little modifications.

## Traditional Uses

Castor leaves are used in Vata and katha, intestinal worms, ear ache it increases biliousness. Oil is used in cathartic aphrodisiac, anthelmintic, back pain, lumbago, convulsions, piles ring worms, paralysis and inflammation.

## Dose

15 to 30 ml before going to bed.

## Storage

In well filled, well closed container in cool place.

## Market Formulations :

1. **Castor oil :** Paras Pharmaceuticals Ltd., Paras House, Ahmedabad - 380014.

2. **Hydrogenated Castor Oil.**

# COCOA BUTTER

## Synonyms

Theobroma oil; Cacao butter.

## Biological Source

It is a fat obtained from roasted seeds of Theobroma cacao L, family Sterculiaceae.

## Geographical Source

Cocoa is cultivated in most of the tropical and sub-tropical countries, especially Sri Lanka, Philippines, Brazil; Curacao, Mexico, Ecuador; West Africa and Western Coast of India.

Cocoa has been used by Mexicans since long time and even was known to Columbus and Cortez. Cocoa butter was prepared as early as 1695 A. D.

## Description of Herb

Coco tree is about 10 metres in height and flowers arise directly from old branches or trunk of the tree and develop into fruits. Fruits are 10 furrowed longitudinally oval in shape, fleshy and yellow to reddish in colour. Fruits contain five rows of seeds and each row contains about 10 - 12 seeds.

Seeds are separated from fruits which are whitish to reddish brown in colour. Seeds are allowed to ferment and get changed to dark brown in colour. The seeds are roasted below 140°C to loose water and also to develop their characteristic flavour and taste.

Roasted seeds are passed through nibbling machine to crack the outer seeds coats. Seed coats (shells) are separated by simple winnowing process. The broken kernels also knownas **nibs** are then ground (churning) between hot rollers, which results to produce coco butter.

## Preparation of Cocoa Butter

Cocoa seeds contain about 50 per cent of cocoa butter. The seeds are separated from pods and are allowed to ferment wherein the seeds change their colour from white to dark reddish-brown due to enzymatic reaction. The fermentation process takes place at 30 - 40°C. The process of fermentation is carried out in boxes or in the cavities made in the earth for 3 - 6 days. After fermentation, the seeds are roasted at 100 - 140°C, which loose water and acetic acid from the seeds and facilitates removal of seed coat. The seeds are then cooled immediately and are fed to nibbling machine to remove the shells followed by winnowing. The kernels are then fed to hot rollers which yield a pasty mass containing cocoa butter. This is further purified to give cocoa butter. The cocoa shells are processed further to yield alkaloids (Theobromine).

## Macroscopic Characters

Cocoa butter is yellowish-white solid and brittle below 25°C. It has pleasant chocolate odour and taste.

It is insoluble in water, but soluble in ether, chloroform, benzene and petroleum ether.

**Fig. 2.4 : Theobromo cacao plant**

## Chemical Constituents

It consists of glycerides of stearic acid (34 per cent), palmitic acid (25 per cent), oleic (37 per cent) acids and small amount of arachidic acid and linoleic acids. The non-greasiness of product is due to its glyceride structure. Cocoa-butter is free of theobromine.

## Chemical Test

Dissolve 1 gm of theobroma oil in 3 ml of ether in a test-tube at a temp of 17°C and immerse the tube in water having the temp of melting ice. The solution does not become turbid or deposit white flexes in less than three minutes after congealing raise the temp to 15°C, a clear liquid is gradually formed.

## Standards of Quality

| | | |
|---|---|---|
| Specific gravity | - | 0.858 - 0.864 |
| Melting point | - | 30 - 35°C |
| Refractive index | - | 1.4637 - 1.4578 |
| Saponification value | - | 188 - 195 |
| Iodine value | - | 35 - 40 |

## Uses

Cocoa butter is used as a base for suppositories and ointments, manufacture of creams and toilet soaps.

## Substitute

Mango kernel oil, which is a solid fat at room temperature and has a melting point of 35°C, is used as substitute for cocoa butter.

## Market Formulations

1. **Palmer's Cocoa Butter :** Formula skin Therapy Oil, Boots Pharmaceuticals Ltd., Parel, Mumbai - 400012.

2. **Vaseline Jelly :** Cocoa butter, Hindustan Unilever Ltd., Unilever House, B. D. Sawant Marg Chakla, Andheri (E), Mumbai 400099.

# KARANJA OIL

## Synonym

Indian beech.

## Biological Source

Karanj-seeds are valuable for their fixed oil, which is the only part, used medicinally.

It is a non-edible semi-drying fixed oil obtained from the seeds of *Pongamia glabra* Vent. family Papilionaceae constituting about 25.0% of the dried seeds.

## Geographical Source

The plant is found throughout India along the streams and rivers, mainly in Andhra Pradesh, Kerala, Madhya Pradesh, Maharashtra and Tamil Nadu. About 12,000 tonnes of oil per annum is produced in Kerala.

## Description of Herb

It is tall almost evergreen tree, bark is soft grey covered with tubercles, leaf lets 5 - 7, opposite, oblong, ovate, acute about 5 - 10 cm in length, flowers blue or purple in axillary recemes, fruits are legumes thick, woody 5 cm long 1 - 2 seeded found along river side, cultivated.

## Macroscopic Characters

Fresh karanja fixed oil from seeds is yellow-orange in colour, but darkens and becomes reddish-brown on age. The oil has peculiar pungent and disagreeable odour and bitter taste.

**Fig. 2.5 : Karanja twig with fruits**

## Chemical Constituents

Karanja seeds contain about 27 per cent of fixed oil. The fatty acid composition of the karanja oil is as follows :

Lignoceric acid    –   1.0 - 3.5 per cent

Oleic acid    –   44 - 75 per cent

Linoleic acid    –   10 - 18.5 per cent

Behenic acid    –   4.0 - 5.5 per cent

Palmitic acid    –   3.5 - 9 per cent

Stearic acid    –   2.5 - 9.0 per cent

Arachidic acid    –   2.2 - 5 percent

Unsaponifiable matter of the oil contains β-sitosterol, and non-fatty components karanjin, karanja chromene, pongapin and pongamol.

## Standards of Quality

Specific gravity    :   0.9273 - 0.930

Refractive index    :   1.4736 - 1.4739

Saponification value    :   181 - 182

Iodine value    :   89 - 90

Acid value    :   6 - 7

Acetyl value    :   21 - 22

Unsaponifiable matter    :   4.2 per cent

## Traditional Use

Karanj oil is used to treat scabies and other skin diseases.

## Uses

karanja oil is used in the treatment of scabies, herpes, leucoderma and other cutaneous diseases. It is also used in rheumatism.

## Market Formulations

1. **Chiropex cream :** Himalaya Drug Co. Makali. Bangalore - 562123.

2. **Vitilo topical liquid :** Elder Pharmaceutical Pvt. Ltd., Andheri (W), Mumbai - 400053.

# LINSEED

## Synonyms

Flax seed, Linum.

## Biological Source

Linseed consists of dried ripe seeds of the plant known as *Linum usitatissimum* Linn. family Linaceae. It contains not less than 25 per cent of fixed oil and not more than 1 per cent of foreign organic matter.

## Geographical Source

Linum is found in Russia, Canada, the U.S.A. and Argentina. In Egypt, Algeria, Italy and Greece, it is cultivated as source of fibres, while in India it is cultivated for fibres as well as oil. Four species of linseed are recorded in India but only Linum usitatissimum is cultivated for its oil content. In India, it is cultivated entirely for the seeds. It is cultivated in Uttar Pradesh, Madhya Pradesh, on a commercial scale.

## Cultivation and Collection

It is cultivated as a Rabbi crop. It needs about 175 cm of rainfall and grows well in black cotton soil. The cultivation is done by sowing the seeds in October and the crop is ready by February/March. Broadcasting method of cultivation is adopted and the distance kept between two rows is about 30 cm. Irrigation and fertilizers are provided according to requirements. Ammonium sulphate and urea are the common fertilizers given to this plant.

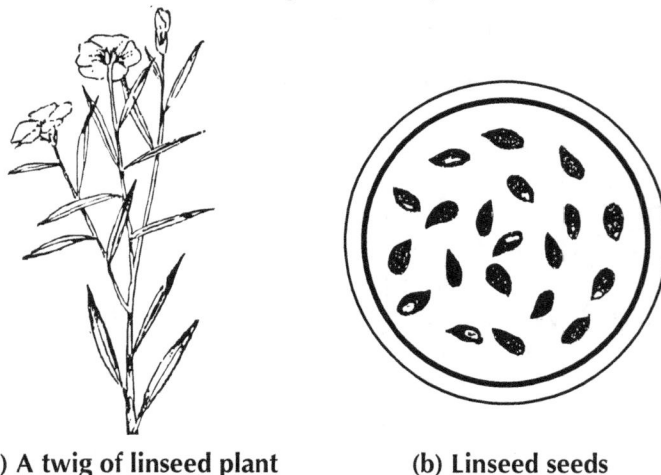

(a) A twig of linseed plant            (b) Linseed seeds

Fig. 2.6

Plants are 40 - 60 cm in height and bear blue coloured flowers. The plants are cut close to the ground. They are allowed to dry for 2 - 3 days and are then thrashed to break the capsules. Seeds coming out are separated by winnowing. The seeds are seived and packed in gunny bags.

## Macroscopic Characters

| | | |
|---|---|---|
| **Colour** | : | Brown |
| **Odour** | : | None |
| **Taste** | : | Mucilaginous and bland |

**Size**      :  Seeds are about 4 - 6 mm in length and 2 - 2.5 mm in width.

**Shape**     :  They are elongated, ovate, strongly flattened, rounded at one end and obliquely pointed at the other.

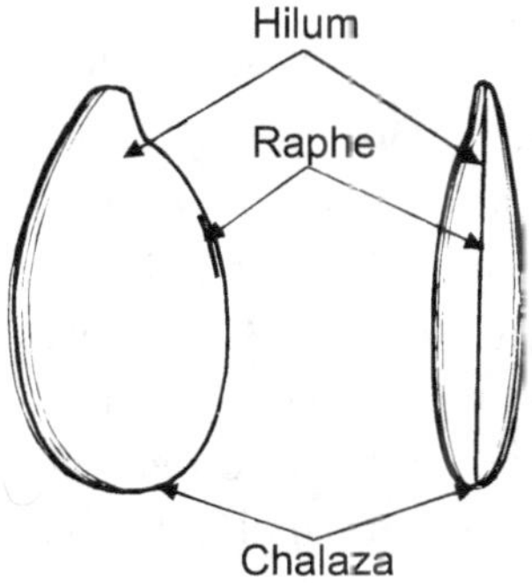

(a) **Front view**          (b) **Side view**

**Fig. 2.7 : Linseed seed**

## Extra Features

Seeds are glossy in appearance. One end has slight depression enclosed in hilum and micropyle. From the hilum yellowish raphe runs to the chalazas.

## Chemical Constituents

Linseed contains about 20 - 40 per cent of fixed oil; 20 per cent of proteins. It also contains mucilage (2 - 7 per cent) and a cyanogenetic glycoside, linamarin. Additionally it contains pectin about 10 per cent and an enzyme linase.

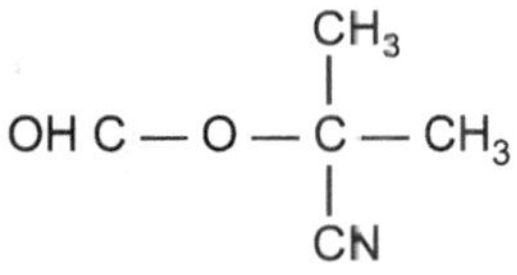

$$OH\ C - O - \underset{\underset{CN}{|}}{\overset{\overset{CH_3}{|}}{C}} - CH_3$$

**Linamarin**

## Standards of Quality

| | |
|---|---|
| FOM | ≯ 2.0 percent |
| Ash | ≯ 5.0 percent |
| Acid insoluble ash | ≯ 1.0 percent |
| WSE | ≮ 15.0 percent |
| Fixed oil | ≮ 30.0 percent |

## Ayurvedic Properties

| | | |
|---|---|---|
| **Rasa** | : | Madhur, Tikta |
| **Guna** | : | Snigdha |
| **Veerya** | : | Ushna |
| **Veepak** | : | Katu |

## Uses

Linseed is used as a source of linseed oil (which is a drying oil) and also as a demulcent. Linseed meal is used as poultice.

# LINSEED OIL

## Method of Preparation of Linseed Oil

The variety yielding high percentage of oil is selected for extraction of oil. Seeds are sieved to make free of earthy matter and other materials.

Commercially, linseed oil is produced by use of expellers. Before the seeds are subjected to the expellers, they are milled into meal, then moistened and heated by means of steam jacketed troughs fitted over the expellers. An average yield of oil is 30 - 35 per cent. The expressed oil is tanked for a long period to settle the colouring matter and mucilage. The oil is then treated with alkali immediately after filtration. Alkali treatment helps to remove free fatty acids. Bleaching of the oil is done by using either charcoal or fueller's earth at elevated temperature. The refined oil so obtained, is chilled to separate wax.

## Macroscopic Characters

| | | |
|---|---|---|
| **Colour** | : | Pale yellow coloured clear liquid. |
| **Odour** | : | Characteristic. |
| **Taste** | : | Pleasant. |

Linseed oil gradually thickens on exposure to air forming a thin transparent film.

It is slightly soluble in alcohol, insoluble in water and miscible with ether, petroleum ether and chloroform.

## Chemical Constituents

Oil contains the glycerides of palmitic, stearic, oleic; linoleic and linolenic acids. The unsaponifiable matter of the oil contains considerable quantities of sterols, tocopherol and squalene. Linseed oil also contain 3-omega fatty acids.

## Standards of Quality

| | | |
|---|---|---|
| **Specific gravity** | : | 0.927 - 0.931 |
| **Refractive index** | : | 1.4786 - 1.4815 |
| **Sap. value** | : | 188- 195 |
| **Iodine value** | : | 160-200 |
| **Acid value** | : | not more than 4 |
| **Unsaponifiable matter** | : | not more than 1.5 |

## Uses

It is the most important drying oil; hence, considerably large quantities are used for paints and varnishes. Medicinally, it is mainly recommended for external applications like lotions and liniments. It is used in treatment of scabies and other skin diseases along with sulphur. Since, it has very high iodine value; it is used in the preparation of non-staining iodine ointment and other products like cresol with soap. It is nutritive and an emollient, too.

Industrially, this oil is used for various purposes such as in the manufacture of soap, linoleum, greases, polishes plasticisers and polymers.

## Caution

To meet the requirements of various industries, different grades and types of linseed oil are available, in the market. Boiled linseed oil dries at a faster rate and forms a smooth and lustrous film. Linseed oil that has been boiled or treated in dryers such as linoleates or resinates of lead, manganese, cobalt or zinc should not be used in medicine.

## Adulterants

Linseed oil is adulterated with boiled linseed oil, cotton seed oil; sunflower oil, rosin, mineral oils, fish oils and mustard oil. Fish oil and rosin is detected by odour while the presence of mineral oils is identified by studying the composition of unsaponifiable matter.

## Market Products

1. **Flax-seed oil capsules :** Paradise Nutrition Inc. 62 Bajaj Bhavan 226 Nariman Point, 8<sup>th</sup> flr., Opp. Inox Theatre, Mumbai - 400021.

2. **Flax-seed oil omega 3, 6, 9 - 60 vegetarian capsules :** Inlife health care, 110A Liberty plaza, Himayat Nagar, Hyderabad - 50029 (A.P.).

# OLIVE OIL

## Synonym

Vergin Olive Oil.

## Biological Source

It is the fixed oil expressed from the ripe fruits of *Olea europoea* Linne, belonging to family Oleaceae.

## Geographical Source

Olive tree, from which the oil is obtained, is native to Palestine and the countries near to Mediterranean sea. It is cultivated in United States and Southern Australia.

Olive oil is very commonly used in various countries along the Mediterranean sea. Among the largest producers of olive oil, Italy, Spain and Greece are the leading countries. The others are United States, Turkey, Tunisia, Morocco and Syria.

## Description of Herb

It is small evergreen tree and attains maximum ten metre height. Olive tree bears drup type of fruits which are normally purple in colour. Fruits also vary in colour, size and yield of oil.

## Method of Preparation of Olive Oil

Oil is obtained by crushing and pressing the peeled pulp which is free of endocarp. The olives consist of 20 - 30 per cent oil and the fruit pulp has 60 - 80 per cent oil. The hydraulic presses are used to squeeze the oil out of fruit under low pressure. This type of technique is called cold pressing and it generates very little amount of heat, because of which it gives the best quality oil called 'virgin olive oil'. The further pressing gives low quality oil. The oil that comes from the last pressing is called olive residue and is generally used for cosmetics, medicines, etc.

## Macroscopic Characters

| | | |
|---|---|---|
| **Colour** | : | Pale yellow or greenish-yellow |
| **Odour** | : | Slight and characteristic |
| **Taste** | : | Bland, faintly acrid |
| **Extra Features** | : | At 10°C it forms pasty mass while at 0°C it becomes solid granular mass. |
| **Solubility** | : | It is slightly soluble in alcohol and miscible with carbon disulphide, chloroform and ether. |

**Fig. 2.8 : Olive tree and fruiting twig**

## Chemical Constituents

The olive oil contains the triglycerides mainly in the form of olein, palmitin and linolein.

Turkish variety contains about 75 % of oleic acid, 10 % palmitic and about 9.0 % lenoleic acid, while Italian variety contains 65 % oleic acid, 15.0 % polmitic acid, hexadecenoic, myrestic acid and arachidic acids are reported in small quantities.

## Chemical Test

Under *ultra-violet* radiation it gives deep golden-yellow colour, while refined oil at gives pale blue fluorescence Discolouring with charcoal removes fluorescence.

## Standards of Quality

Specific gravity        -   0.910 - 0.915 (25°C)

Iodine value            -   79 - 88

Saponification value    -   190 - 195

Free fatty acids        -   The free fatty acids in 10 g require not more than 5 ml 0.1 N sodium hydroxide for neutralisation.

## Uses

Externally, it is an emollient and soothing agent for inflamed surfaces. It is used to soften the skin and crusts in eczema and psoriasis; it is also used as an ingredient of ear wax.

Internally, it is used as nutrient, demulcent and as mild laxative. It is used as a vehicle for oily suspensions for injection.

It is used as setting retardant for dental cements, in the preparation of soaps, liniments and plasters.

## Market Formulations

1.  **Figaro Olive Oil :** Figaro India, 201 Dhanthak Plaza, Makwana Road, Marol Andheri (E), Mumbai 400059.

2.  **Baby Massage Oil :** The Himalaya Drug Co., Makali Bangalore - 562162.

3.  **Extra Vergin Olive Natural Shaving Foam :** Maclyn Naturals, 238 Ravenscliffe Road, Kirup Western Australia 6251.

# SESAME OIL

## Synonyms

Teel oil, Gingelly oil or Benne oil.

## Biological Source

It is fixed oil obtained by expression from the seeds of *Sesamum indicum* family Pedaliaceae.

## Geographical Source

The plant is indigenous to India, and is cultivated in Caribbean islands, China, Japan, Africa and the United States.

## Description of Herb

Sesame herb is an erect pubescent annual, about one metre in height branching from base itself. Leaves are oblong, toothed, green 3 - 5 cm long, sesame plant bears pink or whitish flowers, which are 2 to 3 cm inlength. Fruits of the plant are quadrangular capsules shortly beaked and 2.5 - 3 cm in size. Fruits bear numerous small white or black seeds.

## Method of Preparation

Sesame seeds contain about 50 per cent of fixed oil. Only white variety of seeds is used for pharmaceutical purposes. Seeds are very small in size. They are cleaned, if necessary, washed, sun-dried and expressed to yield oil at room temperature. Subsequently, the temperature and pressure are raised. The oil is purified by refining method and used.

## Macroscopical Characters

| | | |
|---|---|---|
| **Colour** | : | Pale yellowish liquid |
| **Odour** | : | Slight, characteristic |
| **Taste** | : | Bland |
| **Solubility** | : | It is slightly soluble in alcohol, miscible with chloroform, solvent ether, light petroleum (40 - 60 per cent) and carbon disulphide. |

**Fig. 2.9 : Flowering sesame plant**

## Extra Features

It does not solidify at 0°C.

## Chemical Constituents

Gingelly oil contains glycerides of higher fatty acids mainly oleic, linoleic, palmitic, stearic, and arachidic acids. It contains about 5 per cent of olefin, and a phenol known as sesamol which is responsible for stability of oil. It also contains lignin derivatives; sesamin and sesamolin.

**Sesamolin**                    **(+) Sesamin**

### Identification : Badouin's test

Shake 2 ml sesame oil with 1 ml 1 per cent solution of sucrose in hydrochloric acid, a pink or red colour is produced due to sasamol.

Sesame seeds are brain tonic and also improve complexion when applied to skin in the form of crushed meal. Oil has strong healing properties.

## Standards of Quality

| | | |
|---|---|---|
| Weight per ml | : | 0.916 - 0.919 g |
| Refractive index | : | 1.472 - 1.476 |
| Acid value | : | Not more than 2 |
| Iodine value | : | 103 - 116 |
| Saponification value | : | 188- 195 |
| Free fatty acids | : | Not more than 1 per cent |
| Unsaponifiable matter | : | Not more than 1.5 per cent |

## Ayurvedic Properties

| | | |
|---|---|---|
| **Rasa** | : | Madhur |
| **Guna** | : | Snigdha |
| **Veerya** | : | Ushna |
| **Veepak** | : | Madhur |

## Uses

Oil is nutritive, laxative and demulcent; it has got emollient properties. It is used in the preparation of liniments, ointments and soaps, similar to olive oil. Pharmaceutically, it is used as a vehicle for intramuscular oily injections and as a base for ayurvedic oily formulations. After burning, sesame oil yields high quality black ink. Sesame seeds are brain tonic and also improve complexion and applied to skin in the form of crushed meal oil has strong healing properties.

## Market Formulations

1. **Sesame Oil for Massage :** VVS and Sons, New NC 10, Venkateshwara Garden, East Coast Road Kottivakkam, Chennai 600041.

2. **Organic Sesame Oil :** Kama Ayurvedic Pvt. Ltd., 3K, Commercial Circle, Jangpura Extension, New Delhi - 110014.

# BEESWAX

## Synonyms

Yellow Beeswax; Cera-flava

## Biological Source

Yellow beeswax is purified wax and obtained from honey-comb of the bees *Apis dorsata*. *Apis mellifica* and other species of *Apis*, belonging to family Apidae.

## Geographical Distribution

It is processed and commercially prepared in France, Italy, West Africa, Jamaica and India.

## Processing and Preparation for Market

The combs and capping of honey-comb are broken and boiled in soft water. These are then enclosed in a porous bag weighted to keep it under water. The boiling causes oozing of the wax, which collects outside of the bag and forms a cake after cooling. The debris on the outer surface is removed by scraping. Bees wax is purified by heating in boiling water or dilute sulphuric acid and settling. The process is repeated several times and finally wax is skimmed off. Various techniques are adopted to bleach wax, such as treatment with hydrogen peroxide; chromic acid, ozone etc. Sometimes, treatment with charcoal, chlorine or potassium permanganate is also given to bleach the wax. Natural bleaching by exposing the wax to the sun-light in thin layers is also preferred.

## Macroscopic Characters

| | | |
|---|---|---|
| **Colour** | : | Yellow to yellowish-brown. |
| **Odour** | : | Agreeable and honey like. |

**Fig. 2.10 : Honey-bee**

## Extra Features

Yellow bees-wax is non-crystalline solid. It is soft to touch and crumbles under the pressure of fingers to plastic mass. Under molten condition, it can be given any desired shape. It breaks with a granular fracture.

## Solubility

It is insoluble in water, soluble in hot alcohol, ether, chloroform, carbon tetrachloride, fixed and volatile oils.

## Chemical Constituents

The chief constituent of beeswax is myricin i.e. myricyl palmitate (about 80 percent Free cerotic acid $C_{26}H_{53}COOH$ (about 15 %), small quantities of melissic acid and aromatic substance cerolein are the other constituents. Indian beeswax has the acid value of 17 to 22.

## Standards of Quality

| | | |
|---|---|---|
| **Melting point** | : | 60 to 65° C |
| **Specific gravity** | : | 0.958 to 0.967 |
| **Acid value** | : | 5 to 8 |
| **Sap. value** | : | 90 to 103 |
| **Ester value** | : | 80 to 95 |

## Uses

Beeswax is used in preparation of ointments, plasters and polishes. It is used in ointment for hardening purposes in the manufacture of the cancles, moulds and in dental and electronic industries. It is also used in the cosmetics for the preparation of lipsticks and face creams. Pharmaceutically, it is an ingredient of paraffin ointment I.P.

**White bees wax :** Obtained by bleaching yellow bees wax. it should not be used for ophthalmic purposes.

## Adulterants :

Very frequently, beeswax is adulterated with colophony, hard paraffin, stearic acid, Japan wax, spermaceti, carnauba wax and several other substances. Adulteration can be detected on the basis of solubility and melting points. The genuine wax should not give turbidity when 0.5 g of wax is boiled with 20 ml of aqueous caustic soda for 10 minutes and cooled.

## Market Formulations

1. **Beeswax Lip Balm :** Burts Bees Inc., Oakland, California, USA.

2. **Vedic Line Soft Heel Cream :** HVM Network Pvt. Ltd., 395 Shatipur ghat, New Delhi.

3. **Drep Wax Ear Drop :** DWD Pharmaceuticals Ltd., Da amal House, 4th floor, Jamnalal Bajaj Road, Nariman Point, Mumbai - 400021.

# COD LIVER OIL

## Synonym

Oleum morrhi

## Biological Source

It is processed from fresh liver of cod fish, Gadus morrhua and other species of Gadus (family - Gadidae).

## Geographical Source

Large quantities of oil consignments are prepared in coastal regions of Norway, Scotland, Iceland, Germany, Denmark and Britain.

## Cod Fishes - The Source of Vitamin

Cod fishes are about 1.0 to 1.5 metre in length and may weigh from 10.0 to 25.0 kg at times. During January to April they migrate to north coast of Norway for food. They feed on herring and plantation which are the sources of Vitamin D, this Vitamin is conserved in the fat of liver. Gall bladders are removed from liver and oil is extracted from liver taking every care to pressure them properly and keep awy from deterioration of vitamins.

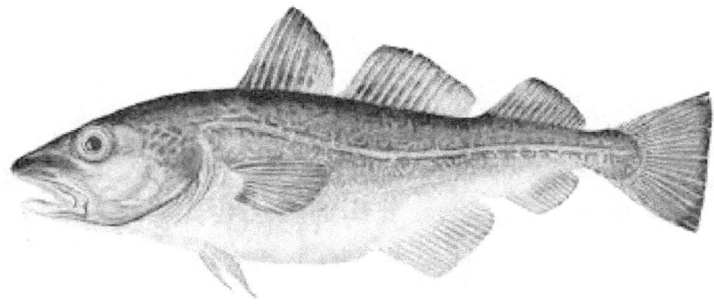

**Fig. 2.11 : Cod fish**

## Method of Preparation

The fishes are caught by nets, opened, and livers are separated. The healthy livers free front gall bladders are washed, minced, steamed in steam jacketed vessels or 'kars' at a temperature not exceeding 85°C for half an hour, cooled and buried in snow for several days. Special barrels are used for this cooling process, which results in separation of stearin. The steaming of oil destroys enzyme lipase. The medicinal oil after filtration is kept in well-closed air tight containers in a cool place protected from light.

Five major steps involved in refining of medicinal cod-liver oil are (a) removal of impurities, (b) drying, (c) winterization, (d) deodorisation, and (e) standardisation for vitamin content. The vitamin A content of the oil is determined spectrophotometrically.

## Description

     **Colour**     :   Pale yellow liquid

     **Odour**      :   Fishy

     **Taste**       :   Bland

## Solubility

It is freely soluble in chloroform, ether, carbon disulphide, petroleum ether, and slightly so e in alcohol.

## Chemical Constituents

The medicinal value of oil is due to vitamin A and vitamin D. About 1 g of oil contains not less than 255 mcg. of vitamin A and 2.125 mcg. of vitamin D. The oil contains glyceryl esters of oleic, linoleic, gadoleic, myristic, palmitic and other acids. Cod liver oil also contains 7 per cent eicosapentaenoic acid and 7 per cent docesahexanoic acid. (Both of them are omega-3 fatty acids).

**Vitamin A**

The oil is used as source of vitamins, as a nutritive and in treatment of rickets and tuberculosis.

**Eicosapentaenoic acid (EPA)**       **Decosahexaenoic acid (DHA)**

As a result of competition from vitamin concentrates, the consumption of medicinal oil has substantially decreased in developed countries of Europe and the USA. The renewed interest in fish liver oils, particularly cod liver oil resulting from nutritional requirements for polyunsaturates in diet, coupled with blood cholesterol reducing property the vistas of trade seem to open ahead for commerce and industry of fish liver oil.

Non-destearinated cod liver oil is the entire oil that has not been chilled to separate stearin. The oil contains not more than 0.5 per cent by volume 'of water and liver tissues and it deposits stearin upon chilling.

**Vitamin D 3 (Cholecalciferol)**

## Standards of Quality

| | | |
|---|---|---|
| **Specific gravity** | : | 0.918 - 0.927 |
| **Refractive index** | : | 1.4705 - 1.4745 |
| **Acid value** | : | less than 2 |
| **Sap. value** | : | 180 - 190 |
| **Iodine** | : | 145 - 180 |

## Uses

It is used as neutritive and specially in patients, suffering from rickets and tuberculosis.

## Traditional Uses

General debility and Tonic

## Storage

In order to avoid loss of vitamins during storage, the oil should be kept in well-filled airtight containers, protected from light and in a cool place. The addition of small quantities of certain antioxidants (e.g. dodecyl gallate) is permitted. It may be bottled in containers from which air has been expelled by production of vacuum or by an inert gas like nitrogen.

## Market Formulations

1.  **Seacod Capsules :** Universal Medicine Pvt. Ltd., Plot No. 815 GIDC, Sarigam Dist. Valsad, Gujarat - 396155.

2.  **Cod Liver Oil Capsules :** CODESOFT, Soft gelatine capsules, Indchemie Health Specialities Pvt. Ltd., 510 Shah and Nahar Industrial Estate Worli Naka, Mumbai 400018.

# SHARK LIVER OIL

**Synonyms :**

Oleum Selachoids

## Biological Source

Shark liver oil is the fixed oil obtained from the fresh and carefully preserved livers of various species of the shark, mainly *Hypoprion brevirostris*. In India, *Scoliodon*, *Carcharias* and *Sphyrna* are abundant among the species, and are generally utilised for the extraction purpose.

According to Indian Pharmaco, one gram of oil should not contain less than 6000 International Units of vitamin A activity.

## Geographical Source

In India, the sharks (Fig.) are processed and oil is obtained on commercial scale in Tamil Nadu, Maharashtra and Kerala. Most of the European countries are also producing shark liver oil on large scale.

## Method of Preparation

With a little variation, the principle involved in extraction of the oil from the livers is uniform in almost all cases. Government factories in Tamil Nadu and Maharashtra process livers for extracting the oil. The livers are cleaned and minced. The minced mass is taken to a boiling pot, where the temperature of 80°C is maintained. The oil extracted is treated with dehydrating agent to remove traces of water.

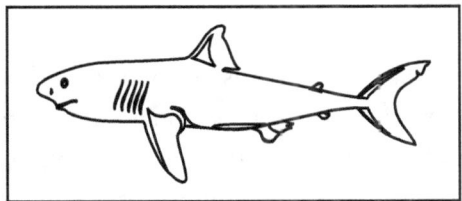

**Fig. 2.12 : Shark Fish (Carcharias Species)**

The oil is then taken to a vacuum still for dehydration and chilled to separate stearin. Centrifuges are used to separate the suspended materials in oil. The clear oil is manipulated to adjust the desired strength. The oil being sensitive to light and air, all the while, care is taken to minimize its exposure to sunlight and air. Many a times, the livers are stored at very low temperature, until they are taken for processing.

## Description

| | | |
|---|---|---|
| **Colour** | : | Pale yellow to brownish-yellow, liquid. |
| **Odour** | : | Characteristic fishy, but not rancid. |
| **Taste** | : | Bland or fishy. |

## Solubility

Shark liver oil is soluble in solvent ether, chloroform and light petroleum. However, it is insoluble in water and slightly soluble in ethyl alcohol.

## Chemical Constituents

Shark liver oil contains vitamin A. The concentration of vitamin A in the oil varies from 15000 to 30000 International Units of vit. A activity per gram. Other constituents of the oil are the glycerides of saturated and unsaturated fatty acids.

## Standards of Quality

The pharmaceutical grade of shark liver oil should comply with the following standards.

| | | |
|---|---|---|
| **Specific gravity** | : | 0.912 to 0.916 |
| **Refractive index** | : | 1.459 to 1.477 at 40° |
| **Acid value** | : | Not more than 2 |
| **Iodine value** | : | Not less than 90 |

## Identification

1. Dissolve one gram of shark liver oil in 1 ml of chloroform and treat with 0.5 ml of sulphuric acid. It acquires light violet colour, changing to purple and finally to brown (due to vitamin A).

2. Dissolve 1.0 ml of shark liver oil in 10 ml of chloroform and treat with saturated solution of antimony trichloride in chloroform. Shake it well. A blue colour is developed (due to vitamin A).

## Uses

It is used in the deficiency of vitamin A. It is also known as *antixeropthalmic factor*. (However, it should be noted that shark liver oil is free of vitamin D and is required to be fortified when necessary. Due to the absence of vitamin D, shark liver oil is not a vitamin substitute for cod liver oil). It is also nutritive. Pharmaceutically, it is used in the preparation of dilute shark liver oil, shark liver oil emulsion (Indian N.F.) and shark liver oil with vitamin D. It is used in burn and sunburn ointments.

## Storage

Shark liver oil is preserved in well-filled and well-closed containers protected from light and in cool place.

## Market Formulations

1. **Sharkoferol :** Alembic Limited, Alembic Road, Vadodara - 390003.

2. **Sharkel Soft Gelatine Capsules :** Elnova Pharma, Nahan Road, Village Muginand Kala Amb, Dist. Sirmour.

3. **Medithane Ointment :** Wyeth Ltd., RBC Mahindra Towers, 4th floor A Wing, Worli, Mumbai - 400018.

# WOOL FAT

## Synonyms

Lanolin, Adeps Lanae

## Biological Source

Hydrous wool fat is the purified fat-like substance obtained from the wool of the sheeps *Ovis aries* Linn. (Family : Bovidae). It contains not less than 20 % and not more than 30 % of water.

## Geographical Source

Commercially, lanolin is manufactured in Australia, U.S.A. and to some extent in India.

**Fig. 2.13 : The Sheep**

## Method of Preparation

Raw wool contains about 31 % wool fibres, suint or wool sweat (chemically potassium salts of fatty acids), about 32% earthy matter and about 25% wool grease or crude-lanolin. Crude lanolin is separated by washing with sulphuric acid or suitable organic solvent or soap solution. It is further purified and bleached. The product is known as anhydrous lanolin or wool fat.

The hydrous wool fat is produced by intimately mixing wool fat with 30.0 % water.

## Description

| | | |
|---|---|---|
| **Colour** | : | Whitish yellow. |
| **Odour** | : | Faint and characteristic. |
| **Taste** | : | Bland. |

## Extra Features

It is found in the form of ointment-like mass and on heating in water bath, water gets separated and it separates into two layers.

## Solubility

It is practically insoluble in water and soluble in chloroform and solvent ether with separation of water.

## Chemical Constituents

Hydrous wool fat contains esters of cholesterol and isocholesterol with carnaubic, oleic, myristic, palmitic, lanoceric and lanopalmitic acids. It also contains 50 % of water.

**Cholesterol**

## Chemical Test

Dissolve 0.5 g of hydrous wool fat in chloroform and to it add 1 ml of acetic anhydride and two drops of sulphuric acid. A deep green colour is produced indicating the presence of cholesterol.

## Standards of Quality :

Anhydrous lanolin (wool fat) has following standards :

| | | |
|---|---|---|
| **Melting point** | : | 34 to 40° |
| **Acid value** | : | Not more than 1.0 |
| **Iodine value** | : | 18 to 32 |
| **Sap. value** | : | 92 to 105 |
| **Ash :** | | Not more than 0.15 % |

## Uses

The lanolin is mainly used as water absorbable ointment base. It is a very common ingredient and base for several water soluble creams and cosmetic preparations. It may also be allergic.

## Adulterants

Mineral fat i.e. soft paraffin is the main adulterant to wool fat, in addition to vegetable fats. It is not attacked by oiling with potassium hydroxide but may be saponified by alcoholic potassium hydroxide.

## Traditional Uses

In ancient times, lanolin had been popularly used as an emollient. Many people of ancient civilizations and today in modern world believe that application of lanolin can enhance hair growth and prevent loss of hairs.

## Market Formulations

1. **Casil Soap :** Biomedica Life Sciences SF₁ Vijay Apartment, 16 School street, Chromepet Chennai - 600044.

2. **Nipcare Cream :** Neon Laboratories Ltd., 140 Damji Shamji Industrial Complex, Mahakali Caves Road, Andheri (E) Mumbai - 400093.

3. **Mysore Sandal Soap :** Karnataka Soaps and Detergents Ltd. - 27, Industrial Suburb, Bangalore - Pune Highway, Bangalore 55.

☝ ☝ ☝

# Chapter 3

# CARBOHYDRATES

## ISAPGOL

**Synonyms**

Isapghula, Isabgol.

**Biological Source**

Isapgol consists of dried seeds of plant *Plantago oveta Faskal*, belonging to family Plantaginaceae.

**Geographical Source**

It is cultivated in Gujrat, Rajasthan, Uttar Pradesh, now-a-days it is also cultivated successfully in Maharashtra.

**Description of Herb**

It is annual herb and cultivated on large scale for exports and fir its medicinal use as safe laxative.

**Leaves**

Green variable in breadth are 7 to 15 cm long ovate or oblong ovate, slightly serrated with three ribs.

**Flowers**

Flowers are minute in form of terminal spikes. They are scattered or crowded.

Spikes are 2.0 to 5.0 cm in length.

**Fruits**

Fruits are 8 to 10 mm long, rounded, the upper half separating like a lid.

**Seeds**

Seeds are pinkish-brown, boat-shaped, with ovate outline shining with reddish brown spot 2.4 to 3.0 mm in length, 1.0 - 1.5 mm.

**Fig. 3.1 : Isapgol plant**

( 3.1 )

## Cultivation

Isapgol is a rabi crop. It is cultivated by broadcasting method, in the month of November. It thrives well in warm and temperate region. It is cultivated in Gujarat extensively for its medicinal use and exports.

## Macroscopic Characters

| | | |
|---|---|---|
| **Colour** | : | Pinkish grey or brown in colour |
| **Odour** | : | None |
| **Size** | : | 10 to 35 mm in length and 1 to 1.75 mm in width |
| **Shape** | : | Ovate, cymbiform |

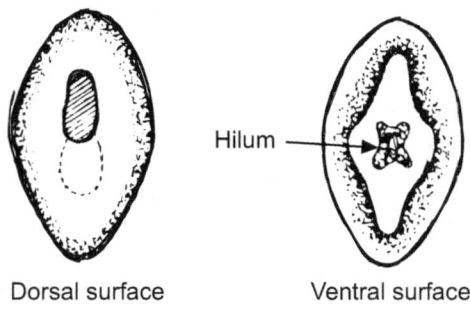

Dorsal surface          Ventral surface

**Fig. 3.2 : Macroscopical characters of isapgol seed**

## Extra Features

Seeds are hard transparent and smooth with grey or reddish brown oval spot in centre of convex surface.

## Chemical Constituents

Husk and seed contains mucilage, chemically it consists of pantosan and aldobionic acid fixed oil and proteins are the other important constituents of the seeds.

## Standards of Quality

For Isapgol husk

| | | |
|---|---|---|
| Total ash | ≮ | 4.5 % |
| Acid Insoluble ash | ≮ | 0.45 % |
| L.O.D. | ≮ | 12.0 % |

## Ayurvedic Properties

| | | |
|---|---|---|
| **Rasa** | : | Madhur |
| **Vipak** | : | Madhur |
| **Veerya** | : | Sheet |
| **Guna** | : | Snigdha, guru, pichil |
| **Doshaghanata** | : | Vata-pitta shamak |

## Traditional Uses

1. Seeds are used in diarrhoea, dysentery and as an emollient.

2. Crushed seeds are used in form of poultice for rheumatic gouty pain.

3. It is also used in infection of bladder, urethra, burning micturation.

4. It is also useful in cases of bronchitis.

## Pharmacological Uses

Seeds are cooling, demulcent, emollient, laxative and diuretic.

Mucilage of isapgol has property of glaizness or stringiness, which is used in certain cosmetic formulations.

## Dosage

5 to 10 gms.

## Substitutes

Several species of plantago are used as substitutes such as

Plantago rhodosperma,

Plantago wrightiana,

Plantago purshil,

Plantago aristata,

Plantago asiatica,

Plantago psyllium.

## Adulterants

*Plantago lanceolata* and *Salvia egyptica* are used as adulterants.

## Market Formulation

1. **Ligaflin :** Aphali Pharmaceutical Ltd., Station Road, Ahmednagar, Maharashtra.

2. **Isapgol :** G India Ltd. Dr. Annie Besant Road, Worli, Mumbai - 25.

3. **Isolax :** Acron Pharmaceuticals, 38/2 Main Road, GIDC Estate, Naroda 382330, Ahmedabad.

# MADHU (MEL)

## Synonyms

Honey.

## Biological Source

Madhu is a sugar secretion deposited in honey comb by the bees, *Apis mellifica, Apis dorsata,* and other species of *Apis,* belonging to family Apidae.

## Geographical Source

Madhu is produced in Africa, Australia, New Zealand, California and India.

## Preparation of Honey by Bees

The nectar of flowers is a watery solution containing 25 % sucrose and 75 % water. The worker bee sucks this nectar through its hollow tube of mouth (proboscis) and deposits in honey-sac located in abdomen. The enzyme invertase present in saliva of the bee converts nectar into invert sugar, which is partially utilised by the bee and the remaining is deposited into honey comb. Honey comb is smoked to remove the bees and honey is obtained by applying pressure to it or allowing it to drain naturally.

The madhu of commerce is heated to 80°C and allowed to stand. The impurities which float over the surface are skimmed off and liquid diluted with water to produce honey of 1.35 density. Natural honey has density of 1.47. Many a times, honey is extracted from the comb by centrifugation. It must be free from foreign substances. Honey is liable to fermentation, unless it is suitably processed. Honey is heated to 80°C before it is sent to market, so as to avoid fermentation. It should be cooled rapidly or else it darkens in colour on keeping. If necessary (and if not prepared by centrifugation method), honey is required to be filtered through wet cloth or flannel.

## Description

| | | |
|---|---|---|
| **Colour** | : | Pale yellow to yellowish-brown. |
| **Odour** | : | Characteristic, pleasant. |
| **Taste** | : | Sweet and faintly acrid. |

## Extra Features

It is syrupy thick liquid, transluscent when fresh and on keeping it becomes opaque and granular due to crystallization of glucose.

## Solubility

It is soluble in water and insoluble in alcohol.

## Chemical Constituents

Honey is an aqueous solution of glucose 35 % (+ 3 %), fructose 45 % (± 5 %) and sucrose about 2 %. The proportion of sugar may vary depending upon source of the nectar and enzymatic activity responsible for converting nectar into honey. The other constituents of honey are maltose, gum, traces of succinic, acid, acetic acid, dextrin and formic acid, colouring matters, enzymes (invertase, diastase, inulase) and traces of vitamins. Proteins and pollen grains from various flowers are also found in honey.

Since, honey is a saturated solution of sugar, on keeping, it starts crystallizing. A product which contains crystallized dextrose is called as Granulated honey. Heating also serves the purpose of minimizing granulation.

## Chemical Test

**Test for reducing sugar :** To the aqueous solution of honey, add Fehlings solution A and B and the reaction mixture is heated on steam both for 30 minutes. Brick red colour is produced due to presence of reducing sugars.

## Standards of Quality

| | | |
|---|---|---|
| **Weight per ml** | : | 1.35 to 1.36 g |
| **Specific rotation** | : | + 3° to − 10° |
| **Total ash** | : | 0.1 to 0.8 % |

## Ayurvedic Properties

| | | |
|---|---|---|
| **Rasa** | : | Madhur |
| **Guna** | : | Laghu, Ruksha |
| **Veerya** | : | Sheetal |
| **Vipak** | : | Katu |

## Uses

Honey is used as a demulcent and sweetening agent. It is readily assimilated and more accepted by the stomach and hence, is a good nutrient to infants and patients. It is antiseptic and applied to burns and wounds. It is a common ingredient of several cough mixtures, cough drops and a vehicle for ayurvedic formulations. Recently, it is used in the preparation of creams, lotions, soft drinks and candies.

Since, ancient times Ayurveda is using honey as a medium for administration of herbal bitter drugs and also as sweeting agent.

## Traditional Uses

For centuries together it is used as sweetening agent in medicaments and also as nutritive for seniors.

## Market Formulation

1.  **OLBAS Cough Syrup :** Olbus Herbal remedies, Philadephia, USA.

✐ ✐ ✐

# Chapter 4
# MIXED CHEMICAL CONSTITUENTS

## ARTEMISIA

### Synonyms

Sweet wormwood

### Biological Source

It consists of dried aerial parts of plant *Artemisia annua* Linn. belonging to family Compositae.

### Geographical Source

It is widely distributed in the temperate, cool temperate and subtropical zones (mainly in Asia) of the world. It is native to China also found in Europe, North Africa, South and South-West Asia.

It is small evergreen erect annual shrub grows upto 30 - 100 cm high.

### Macroscopic Characters

| | | |
|---|---|---|
| **Colour** | : | Green |
| **Odour** | : | Characteristic bitter |
| **Taste** | : | Characteristic, aromatic |
| **Shape** | : | Fern leaves like ovate, twise or thrice pinnatley cut, their lobules oblong - lanceolate, short-acuminate, entire. |

**Fig. 4.1 : Twigs of Artemisia annua herb**

### Extra Features

Leaves are sessile, smaller and less compound; uppermost leaves bracteal, simple with fewer lateral lobes. It bears tiny green-yellow flowers in clusters, stems are cylindrical

### Chemical Constituents

It consists of volatile and non-volatile constituents. The main non-volatile antimalarial chemical constituents of A. annua is sesquiterpenoids - artemisin, other sesquiterpenoids includes artemisinin I, II, III, IV, and V. It also contains artemisinic acid, arteether artemisilactone, and artemisinol. The aerial parts of plant contains camphene, 1-camphor, β-caryophyllene β-pinene and isoartemisia ketone as component of volatile oil (0.2 - 0.25 %).

**Artemisinin**          **Artemisinic acid**

## Ayurvedic Properties

| | | |
|---|---|---|
| Rasa | : | Tikta |
| Guna | : | Laghu, raksha |
| Veerya | : | Ushna |
| Vipak | : | Katu |

## Traditional Uses

1. Commerically, the plant used as source of potent new natural antimalarial compound artemisinin.

2. Artemisinin is widely used as antimalarial against susceptible and multi-drug resistant plasmodium spp.

3. Current research also shows that artemisinin drugs are effective against Cancer, Leishmania, Trypanosoma and some viruses.

4. Poor solubility of artemisinin limit is effectiveness, to overcome it semisynthetic derivatives of artemisinin have been developed. These include, Artesunate, artemether, dihydro-artemisinin, artelinic acid and artemotil.

## Uses

1. In China an infusion of the leaves used internally to treat fever, colds, and diarrhea while externally poultice is being applied for nosebleeds and abscesses, and to treat haemorrhoids and vaginitis.

2. Traditionaly in China, it is used to treat fevers and haemorrhoids.

3. According to traditional Chinese medicine, A. annua controls heat for the alternating fever and chills of malarial disorders.

4. It is also used as a source of essential oils for the perfume industry.

## Storage

It should be stored in well closed well filled containers away from light and in cool place.

# BALA

## Synonyms

Country Mallow.

## Biological Source

It consists of dried roots, leaves and seeds of plant *Sida cordifolia* Linn belonging to family (Malvaceae).

## Geographical Source

It is common roadside plant found throughout India and Nepal upto an altitude of 1050 m. The plant generally grows in damp places Haryana, Uttar Pradesh, Madhya Pradesh.

## Description of Herb

Bala is annual and much branched. It is an erect, bushy perennial, densely pubescent reaches 50 to 200 cm height. The entire plant is covered with soft white felt-like hairs. The stems are yellow-green, hairy, long and slender. The flowers are dark yellow, sometimes with a darker orange center, with a hairy 5-lobed calyx and 5-lobed corolla, the root and stem grow big and strong. The fruit is depressed globose fruits are reticulated with two awns are schizocarpous seeds are smooth.

## Cultivation and Collection

This plant is not cultivated on commercial scale to any extent, but is fully collected from wild grown plants.

## Macroscopic Characters - (Leaves)

| | | |
|---|---|---|
| **Colour** | : | Yellowish green |
| **Odour** | : | Characteristic |
| **Taste** | : | Characteristic |
| **Size** | : | 3.5 × 7.5 to 2.5 to 6 cm |
| **Shape** | : | Oblong ovate heart shaped |
| **Extra Features** | : | Simple, alternate with obtuse apex, serrate crenate margin and hairy |

**Fig. 4.2 : Bala herb**

## Chemical Constituents

The plant contains alkaloids such as β-phenethylamine, ephedrine, pseudo-ephedrine, hypaphorine, vasicinone, vasicinol, choline and betaine. It also shows traces of sitosterol, flavones and palmitic, stearic and hexacosanoic acid, Seeds contain more alkaloids.

**Ephedrine**          **β-Phenethylamine**          Betaine

## Standards of Quality

| | | |
|---|---|---|
| LOD | ≯ | 11.0% |
| Total ash | ≯ | 3.5% |
| Acid insoluble ash | ≯ | 0.5% |
| Water soluble extractives | ≮ | 5.0% |
| Alcohol soluble extractives | ≮ | 2.5% |

## Ayurvedic Properties

| | | |
|---|---|---|
| **Rasa** | : | Madhura |
| **Guna** | : | Guru, snigdha, pichil |
| **Veerya** | : | Sheeta |
| **Vipak** | : | Madhura |

## Pharmalogical Uses

- **Antihypertensive :** A decrease in both heart rate and blood pressure.
- **Antiobesity :** Weight loss is through its hypoglycemic (blood sugar lowering) activity.
- **Analgesic and anti-inflammatory :** It increases pain tolerance and appears to have anti-inflammatory action.
- **Hepatoprotective :** Fumaric acid phenolic compound showed heptatoprotective ability.
- It has strong adoptogen and anti-microbial activity, wound healing and anti-diabetic property.

## Traditional Uses

- The drug held a great repute in Ayurvedic system of medicine for the treatment of rheumatism and used as main ingredient in widely used ayurvedic formulations such as Kirabala, balaritam, rasnadi kayasam, asvagandhaditailam etc. four varieties namely, bala, atibala, nagabala and mahabala are mentioned in standard Ayurveda books (Bhavaprakash Nighantu); among all bala is most widely used.

- Bala is one of the most widely used rasayana tonic herb, after ashwagandha. It is tonic to vata. The sweet, cold, heavy herb that builds immune functions.

- In combination with ashwagandha milk decoction it is recommended in paralysis.

- It is used vata related nervine disorders, additionally it can be used for other organs with combination of specific herbs such as for heart problems it combination with arjuna. The herb also has ability to enhance quality and quantity of reproductive fluid (Shukra Dhatu) for healthy conception. It contains ephedrine and like alkaloids which gives energetic feeling it should cautiously used in hypertension. It is used as anti-inflammatory, bronchodilator for asthma.

- Externally used as medicated oil in joint complaints, frozen shoulder, sciatica, muscle crams and nervine pain.

## Therapeutic Uses

- The plant is alternative tonic, astringent, emollient and aphrodisiac.

- **Bark :** Considered as cooling. It is useful in blood, throat, urinary system related troubles, piles, phthisis and insanity.

- The seeds are considered as aphrodisiac.

- **Roots** are regarded as cooling, astringement, stomachic tonic, aromatic, bitter and diuretic.

- It has a depressant rather than a stimulant effect on the Central Nervous System.

- It may decrease both blood pressure and heart rate.

- It has a hypoglycemic (blood sugar lowering effect).

- It increases pain tolerance.

- It has an anti-inflammatory and antioxidant effect.

## Dosage

Dose 250 mg to 1 gm as decoction, milk decoction or powder, externally as medicated taila.

## Market Formulations

Kirabala,

Balaritam,

Rasnadi Kayasam,

Asvagandhadi Tailam.

# BENAFSHA

## Synonym

Sweet violet, Wild violet.

## Biological Source

It consists of dried aerial parts obtained from *Viola odorata* Linn, belonging to family Violaceae. The drug is collected in April and May, when it is in flowering. It is dried on tarpaulin sheets and dried in the shade.

## Geographical Source

Sweet violet is indigeneous to India and found in Kashmir (kangra), Himachal Pradesh (Chamba), and Kamaon hills, Baramulla, Udhampur, Kistauar, Manali, Kullu and Amritsar.

## Cultivation and Collection

Benafsha is cultivated only in gardens. Its cultivationi s also undertaken in hilly regions of North India. It grows quite satisfactorily in cool and moist climatic conditions. It does not survive on exposure to heavy rains. Its propagations can be done either by cutting or with seeds. Drug is actually found at an altitude of 1500 - 1800 m. For medicinal purpose it is collected from April to July.

## Description of Herb

Benafsha is a glabrous or pubescent herb, about 15 cm, in height. Its root stocks are very stout and stolons are cylindrical. Leaves are dark green, tough, broadly ovate or cordate inshape with crenate margin. They are 1.5 - 5 cm in size. Flowers are solitary, auxillary forming central flowering rosettes. Flowers are very beautiful in colour. They are deep violet in shade with bluish-white base. Flowers are sweet, scented and which is why the plant is cultivated in gardens as an ornamental crop. Fruits are in the form of capsules, round, three angled and often purplish in colour. The plant blooms in second year.

**Fig. 4.3 : Viola odorata herb**

The drug benafsha in the market is available in different forms, which constitute various aerial parts of plant.

1. Kashmiri benafsha    -   Aerial parts like stems, leaves and flowers

2. Gul-i-benafsha       -   Only dried flowers

3. Berg benafsha        -   Aerial parts without flowers

## Chemical Constituents

The leaves are found to contain an essential oil, alkaloid and a colouring matter. It has a very agreeable flavour and is used for high grade perfumes. The root stocks contain saponins, a glycoside of methyl salicylate responsible for expectorant property, an essential oil, and alkaloid odoratine. Flowers contain a substance known as violine, volatile, oil, rutin and cyanin. It contains 0.1 per cent concentrate responsible for highly pleasant odour of the drug.

Odoratine

## Ayurvedic Properties

| | | |
|---|---|---|
| **Rasa** | : | Madhur, tikta |
| **Guna** | : | Snigdha |
| **Veerya** | : | Sheetal |
| **Vipak** | : | Madhur |

## Uses

The herb is used as expectorant, diaphoretic and antipyretic. The herb shows antibacterial and antifungal activities, and hence used in the treatment of eczema. It is used in the form of *sarbat*. The flowers are emollient, demulcent and are said to relieve pain due to cancerous growth. The leaves and stems in large doses are cathartic. Violine is an emetic.

## Traditional Uses

Fresh leaves are reputed for the treatment of cancer and relieve cancerous pain. In the form of flower infusion it is used for liver disorders.

# CHITRAK

## Synonyms
White lead wart.

## Biological Source
It consists of dried matured root bark of Plant *Plumbago zeylanica* Linn. belonging to family Plumbaginaceae.

## Geographical Source
It is commonly found as ornamental plant throughout India and Asia.

## Description of Herb
The plant is a long lived and reaches to a height of 1 - 2.5 metres.

**Stem**     : Thin, round, nodular and delicate having vertical striations.

**Leaves**  : Oval shaped resembling bilva leaves, 10 cm long, 4 cm broad.

**Flowers** : Stalk of flowers is branched and 10 - 20cm long. Plant Flowers in winter season.

**Fruits**    : Itbears legumes with sticky covering and oval in shape. Fruiting is just after a month of flowering season.

**Seeds**    : Each fruit has one oval seed.

**Roots**    : Finger-like thick, red from outside but white inside, flexible like shatavari.

**Fig. 4.4 : Chitrak herb with flowers**

## Macroscopic Characters

**Color**          : Outer reddish to deep brown, inner white.

**Odour**         : Disagreeable

**Taste**          : Acrid and bitter

**Shape**         : Cylindrical

**Size**            : Roots 30 cm or more in length, 6 mm or more in diameter as also as short stout pieces.

**Extra feature** : Shows presence of scars of rootlets present, bark is thin, internal structure striated.

**Fig. 4.5 : Chitrak roots**

## Chemical Constituents

Roots contain bitter crystalline yellow needle-like glycosidal active substance, naphthoquinones - plumbagin. It also contains 3-biplumbagin, chloroplumbagin, chitranone, elliptone.

The coumarins seselin, 5-methoxyseselin, suberosin and xanthyletin. Other compounds were 2, 2-dimethyl-5-hydroxy- 6-acetylchromene, plumbagin acid, sitosterol, β-sitosteryl-glucoside, akuchiol, 12-hydroxyisobakuchiol, saponaretin, isoorientin, isoaffinetin and psorealen.

**Plumbagin**

## Ayurvedic Properties

| | | |
|---|---|---|
| **Rasa** | : | Katu (pungent) |
| **Guna (qualities)** | : | Laghu (lightness), Rooksha (dryness) Teekshna (piercing, strong) |
| **Veerya** | : | Ushna (hot potency) |
| **Vipaka** | : | Katu - undergoes pungent taste conversion after digestion. |
| **Effect on Tridosha** | : | Because of its hotness, it balances Vata and Kapha Doshas. |

## Pharmacological Use

In preclinical studies roots of chitrak shown potent immunomodulatory, antioxidant, anticancer, anti-inflammatory, Antidiabetic and antimalarial. effect. It also shown positive effect in CNS studies. Additionally alcoholic extract shown antimicrobial and antiviral effect in in-vitro studies.

## Traditional Uses

- It stimulates digestion, act as bitter tonic, increases digestion and vitiates blood; hence useful in bowel disorders, de-worming and for dysentery.
- It is good for lucoderma, piles, bronchitis and vata and kapha vitiation cases, kandu, ascitus.
- It induces uterine contractions and induces abortion.
- It also act as antiantheminitic, prevents expulsion of excess malas.
- Effective in liver and spleen disorders. Leaves are aphrodisiac, good for scabies.

**Dosage :** 0.4-1.6gm

## Market Formulations

1. **Chitrak Haritaki :** Used in chronic respiratory conditions (Dabur, Gaziabad, Uttar Pradesh.
2. **Chitrakadi vati :** Used in indigestion (Patanjali Ayurved Limited, Haridwar, Uttarakhand - 249401)
3. **Kalyanagulam :** Used in liver and skin conditions. (Arya Vaidya Sala, Kottakkal, Malappuram (Dist.), Kerala - 676 503,)

## Precautions

Excess use of roots causes toxic signs and poisonous effect and to counter this one has to use pitta-pacifying medications.

# COLOCYNTH

## Synonyms

Bitter apple, Bitter cucumber, colocynth pulp.

## Biological Source

It consists of dried pithy pulp of ripe fruits of *Citrullus colocynthus* Schrador, family Cucurbitaceae, containing not more than 2% of epicarp and 5% of seeds.

## Geographical Source

It is native of Asia, and found in Syria, also in Egypt. It is cultivated in Spain, Sicily and Morocco. It occurs throughout India growing wild, particularly in Tamil Nadu, Gujarat, Punjab and Andhra Pradesh. On dry sandy banks of rivers, lakes and sea beaches.

## Description of Herb

It is a prostate herb with perennial root and simple or 2 fid tendrils, leaves are 2 to 4 cm. Pale green above and ashy beneath, 3 to 4 lobed, corolla is yellow.

**Fig. 4.6 : Colocynth, fruit and herb**

## Cultivation and Collection

It is not cultivated commercially. It is annual or perennial herb with climbing stem. It bears spherical fruits which are green in colour and turn to yellow when matured. Fruits are about 8 to 10 cm in diameter.

The fruits are collected from wild grown plants in autumn, peeled with sharp instruments and dried in the sun. The dried pulp of the full grown fruits, free of rind which constitutes the drug. It is marketed either as broken pieces which are light and spongy or in the form of flakey powder, which is yellowish orange to yellowish green in colour. Pulp of the fruits contains about 15%, seeds about 60% and rest covered by rind.

## Macroscopic Characters

| | | |
|---|---|---|
| **Colour** | : | The fruit is yellowish |
| **Odour** | : | Characteristic |
| **Taste** | : | Intensely bitter |
| **Size** | : | Entire fruits are upto 10 cm in diameter |
| **Shape** | : | Sub-spherical, globular. |

## Extra Features

The berries contain number of seeds which are about 6 × 4 × 2 mm in size, ovoid, flattened and yellowish brown in colour.

## Ayurvedic Properties

| | | |
|---|---|---|
| **Rasa** | : | Tikta |
| **Guna** | : | Laghu, rooksha, teekshna |
| **Veerya** | : | Ushna |
| **Vipak** | : | Katu |

## Chemical Constituents

The principles of the colocynth include bitter amorphous alkaloids and resin. Both of them are responsible for its purgative action. The pulp also contains α-elaterin (also known as Cucurbitacin E). Cucurbitacin L, a glycosidal compound, phytosterol and fatty acids.

**Cucurbitecin (α-elaterin)**

## Standards of Quality

| | |
|---|---|
| Total ash | ⊬ percent |
| Acid insoluble ash | ⊬ 4.0 percent |
| Seeds | ⊬ 5.0 percent |
| Epicarp | ⊬ 2.0 percent |
| Petroleum ether soluble extractive | ⊬ 3.0 percent |

## Uses

It is used as hydragogue purgative being very powerful purgative it is prescribed along with carminatives. The constituents also exhibit necrotic actions.

# DHATAKI PUSHPA

## Synonyms

Dhayati, Tamra pushpa

## Biological Source

This consists of dried flowers of *Woodfordia fruiticosa* Linn., *Woodfordia floribanda* Salib and *Lythrum fruticosum* Linn, Family Lythraceae.

## Geological Source

It is found through out North India upto an attitude of 1500 m and in Baluchistan. It is also cultivated for its ornamental flowers.

It is collected mainly in UP, MP, Himachal Pradesh and Uttarakhand.

## Macroscopic Characteris

It is a medium sized tree with red fascicled axillary racemes. It is normally available in gardens as ornamental herb for beautiful flowers. It has no odour and has characteristic bitter and astringent taste.

**Fig. 4.7 : Dhataki Pushpa herb**

## Cultivation and Collection

It is collected when the plant is under intense flowering and is quickly dried in shade. It flowers during February and April. It is not cultivated on commercial scale and collected only from wild grown plants.

## Chemical Constituents

Dhatakipushpa contains chemically

| | | |
|---|---|---|
| **Tannins** | : | Woodfordin A, ellagic acid, camellin B and nobotannin - I |
| **Flavanoids** | : | Quercetin, naringenin and camellin - B |
| **Anthraquinone** | : | Chrysophanol |
| **Sterols** | : | Hecogenin, β-sitosterol |

**Woodfordin A**

## Traditional Uses

Dhataki pushpa is actually 'Sandhana dravya', i.e. responsible for fermentation process. It enhances fermentation and promote formation of alcohol. Hence, it is indispensable ingredient of all Asavas and Arishtas.

It is uterine tonic, anthelmintic, it is also used in vata and kapha. It has also shown anti-tumour and anti-inflammatory activities.

## Market Ayurvedic Formulations

Kanakasav, Javakarishta, Chandanarishta, Arvindarishta, Drakashrishta, and Ashwagandha rishta.

# KALIJIRI

## Synonyms

Aranya jiraka, Vanjiraka

## Biological Source

It consists of dried leaves fruits and seeds of Centratherum anthelminticum Kuntze. (*Vernonia anthelmintica wild.*) family: asteraceae.

## Geographical Source

Found throughout India upto 2000 m in Himalaya and Sri Lanka.

## Description of Herb

It is widely used in the preparation of Ayurvedic system of medicine and is distributed widely in India, even to the heights of 1800 metres. Certain other plants such as *Nigella sativa* and *Bunium persicum* Boiss are also known as kalajiri or black cumin in India, but even than these three species are still called black cumin or kalajiri.

**Fig. 4.8 : Kaliri fruits**

It is a roubust branched glandular-pubiscent annual plant reaches up to the highet of one to two meters.

**Leaves:** 8 - 20 cm membranous, lanceolate or ovate-lanceolate, coarsely serrate.

**Flower:** Purplish tips with linear involucral bract of 0.5 - 1.0 cm diameter.

## Macroscopic Characters - (Leaves)

| | | |
|---|---|---|
| **Colour** | : | Light green |
| **Odour** | : | Characteristic |
| **Taste** | : | Bitter |
| **Size** | : | 5 to 6 × 2.5 to 3 cm |
| **Shape** | : | Laueclate on elliptic lanceolate, Apex is acute coarsely serrate pubescent on both surfaces |

## Fruits (Achne)

Fruits of about 2 mm in size, narrowed towards base, ten ribbed, black in colour, hairy, hairs are deciduous.

## Chemical Constituents

The main constitutent is delta-7-avenasterol. The bitter principle present in seed is a demanolide lactone. The two novel compounds a flavone glycoside and 8, 5'-dimethoxy 3', 4'-methylenedioxy 3, 7-dihydroxy flavones has been isolated. It also shown the presence of pentacyclic hederagenin triterpenoids such as hederagenin (3-0-[6-Dglucopyronosyl-(l $\rightarrow$ 3)-$\alpha$-L-rhomnopyronosyl-(1 $\rightarrow$ 2)-$\alpha$-L-orabinopyronosyl]-28-0-[6-D-glucuronopyronosyl-(l $\rightarrow$ 4)-$\alpha$-L-rhamnopyranosyl-(l$\rightarrow$3)-6-Dglucopyronosyl] hederogenin). It also showed the presence of stigmesterol and sitosterols. Additionally seed oil shown the presence of unsaturated and saturated fatty acids and little amount of proteins.

The centratherin and germacranolide are present in seeds and leaves.

## Uses

### Ayurvedic Properties

| | | |
|---|---|---|
| **Rasa** | : | katu; tikta |
| **Guna** | : | Laghu, tikshna, |
| **Veeryo** | : | Ushna |
| **Vipak** | : | katu |

### Pharmacological Uses

- Seed alcohol extracts has analgesic, antipyretic and diuretic activity.
- Moderately polar extracts of seed exhibited antifilarial property against S. cervi and S. digitata.
- Seeds extracts found as effective antihelmintic agent in vitro and in vivo studies.
- Plant shown to posses antihyperglycemic activity due to polyphenolic content.
- Plant reported to posses antimicrobial property.
- Clinical studies validates the uses of the drug in skin diseases.
- The drug exhibited smooth muscle relaxant and hypotensive activity in animals.

### Traditional Uses

- Kapha vat shamak, sathahar, badana sthapan, krimighan, Kustaghan, dipan, vaman kayak, rakt sodhak, jwaraghana.
- Traditionally medicine used for fever, cough and as general tonic.
- It is also used for anthelmintic, diuretic, digestive and febrifugal property.
- It also known to be effective in kidney disorders.
- Seeds are used as anthemintic, tonic, stomachic and diuretic.

### Dose

0.1-0.2 gm of seeds or 25-30 ml of infusion

### Marketed Formulations

**Raktapura** capsule (anti acne)

**Gastrex tablet :** A product of (Ban lab India).

### Storage

In well closed containers away from light in cool places.

# KUSHTA

The drug kushta has been mentioned in veda's. It is claimed to cure several diseases and posses the properties like Rasayana, vrushya and krimigna.

## Synonyms

Costus

## Biological Source

It consist of dried roots of plant *Soussurea leppa or S. costus* belonging to family Asteraceae.

## Geographical Source

It is distributed in North Western Himalayas from Kashmir to Kumaon at 2100 - 3900 m altitude.

## Description of Herb

The plant is a slender perennial herb 60 - 150 cm tall with stout thick roots. Stem is stout and fibrous. Leaves arc radical with long winged stalks. Flower heads are stalkless and very hard. Flowers are dark blue purple in auxiliary or terminal clusters. Fruit is an achene.

**Fig. 4.9 : Kushta herb**

## Cultivation and Collection

Due to over exploitation, it is categorized as criticaly endangered for N. W. Himalayas. Cultivation requires a cool and humid climate as in high elevations of 2500 - 3000 m. A deep rich porous soil is preferred, it is successfully cultivated in semi natural condition in Kashmir and Garhwal.

Plant is propagated through seeds or root cuttings. Chilling the seeds for 60 days and gibberlic acid treatment at 20 ppm improved germination. Seeds are propgated in nursery beds in spring and seedlings after sufficient height transplanted in open field at distance of 90 - 90 cm. the roots are collected and made in to pieces of 10 cm and dried.

## Macroscopic Characteristics

| | | |
|---|---|---|
| **Colour** | : | Grey to dull brown |
| **Odour** | : | Strong aromatic |
| **Taste** | : | Bitter |
| **Size** | : | 7-15 cm × 1-1.5 cm |
| **Shape** | : | Cylindrical |

**Fig. 4.10 : Kushta root**

## Extra Feature

Roots are thick and stout occasionally wrinkled. Fracture is short and horny.

Acid group, 13-sulfo-dihydrosantamarine and 13-sulfodihydroreynosin, were isolated

## Chemical Constituents

Kushta contains 18% inulin, 6% of resinoids, 1.5% of essential oil and 0.5% of alkaloids. Besides these constituents roots also found to contains tannins and fixed oil. Essential oil mainly comprised of oil is comprised mostly of sesquiterpene lactones, including dihydrocostus lactone (15%) and costos lactone (10%), other constituents including aplotaxene (20%), d-costen (6%), l-costen (6%), and costic acid (14%), as well as smaller amounts of camphene, phellandrene, caryophyllene and selinene, the major alkaloid reported as saussurine. It is also reported to have the presence of pregnenolone, β-sitosterol, daucosterol. Five new amino acid-sesquiterpene adducts, viz. Saussureamines A, B, C, D and E has been reported. Two new sesquiterpene lactones with the unusual sulfonic acid group, 13 sulfo-dihydro-santamarine and 13 sulfo-dihydrorenocin were isolated.

## Standards of Quality

| | | |
|---|---|---|
| F.O.M. | ⊁ | 2.0% |
| Total ash | ⊁ | 9.0% |
| Acid insoluble | ⊁ | 3.0% |
| A.S.E. | ⊀ | 12% |
| W.S.E. | ⊀ | 28.0% |

## Ayurvedic Properties

| | | |
|---|---|---|
| **Rasa** | : | Tikta, katu, madhura |
| **Guna** | : | Lagu, ruksha, thikshana |
| **Veerya** | : | Ushna |
| **Vipaka** | : | Katu |
| **Doshagnatha** | : | Vata, kaphahara. |

## Phramacolgocial Uses

- Delactonized oil and lactone fractions exhibited antispasmodic activity; furthermore these fractions exhibited hypotensive effect in anaesthetized dogs the effect is due to direct peripheral vasodilation and cardiac depression.

- Different lactone fractions of root showed antihistaminic in experimental animals.

- Costunolide from roots of Saussurea costus showed the possible calcium antagonistic action.

- The ant inflammatory effect of methanolic and ethanolic extract in acute and chronic inflammation was reported.

- The roots of Saussurea reported to posses antioxidant, anticancer, hepatoprotective, anti-ulcer, immunomodulatory, hypolipidemicm hypoglycaemic, antimicrobial activity

## Traditional Uses

- The roots are used mainly as an antispasmodic in asthma, cough and also in treatment of cholera, chronic skin diseases and rheumatism.

- Its different preparations are also used byAyurvedic physicians for the treatment of various ailments like cough and cold, quartan malaria, leprosy, persistant hiccups, rheumatism, hair-wash, stomachache, toothache, typhoid fever, etc.

- It is an important medicine for gout, erysipelas and promotes spermatogenesis.

- The root is also used in Tibetan medicine where it is considered to have an acrid, sweet and bitter.

- Taste with a neutral potency. Several traditional Tibetan formulae that are used for chronic inflammation of the lungs, cough, chest congestion.

## Dose

- Powder : 1-2 gm.

## Market Formulation

1. **Ealaadi Keram :** Nagarjuna Herbal Concentrates Ltd, Kalayanthani PO, Thodupuzha, Kerala 685 588.

2. **Somraji Tail :** Shree Baidyanath Ayurved Bhawan Pvt. Ltd. Kolkata, West Bengal.

3. **Vatha Samana Thailam :** Arya Vaidya Pharmacy, 326, Perumal Koil Street, Ramanathapuram P.O. Coimbatore - 641045, Tamil Nadu.

# MALKANGANI

## Synonyms

Jyotishmati

## Biological Source

Jyotishmati is an ancient Ayurvedic herb, used for its immense health benefits. It consists of seeds of plant *Celastrus paniculatus* Willd. It belongs to family Celastraceae.

## Geographical Source

The plant grows throughout India at elevations up to 1800 m.

## Description of Herb

- Celastrus *paniculatus* is large woody, climbing shrub, up to 10 centimetres in diameter and ten metres long with rough, pale brown exfoliating bark covered densely with small, elongated lenticels.

- The leaves are simple, ovate, oblong-elliptic, nearly circular or obovate or elliptic in shape, with toothed margins.

- Flowers unisexual, small, greenish-white or yellowish-green, in terminal pendulous panicles.

- The capsular fruits are 1-1.3 cm in diameter, depressed, globose, trilobed, bright yellow, 1-6 seeded.

- Seeds are completely enclosed in an orange red aril. It has unpleasant odour and taste.

## Cultivation

*Celastrus panniculatus* can be propagated by seeds. However seed germination is very poor if sown directly without any pre-sowing treatment. As such it can grow in verity of soil, but best grown is in drained soil. Soil should be prepared with repeated ploughed and mixing farmyard manure. The seeds are sown at the distance of two feet on prepared furrow in mid of June or after first rain. Usually the 4 Kg per hector seeds are required. The plant can successfully grow with minimum water supply, it requires irregulation immediately after sowing and next after 15 days interval. Seeds should be picked when they will turn into red colour and dry. They should be dried under sunlight for 7 - 10 days.

Seeds should be soaked in solution of any growth regulators which improve the germination.

## Macroscopic Characteristics

| | | |
|---|---|---|
| **Color** | : | Yellowish or orange red |
| **Odour** | : | Unpleaseant |
| **Taste** | : | Unpleasant |
| **Size** | : | 1.5 - 2.0 mm |

**Shape**    :    Ellipsoidal or oval

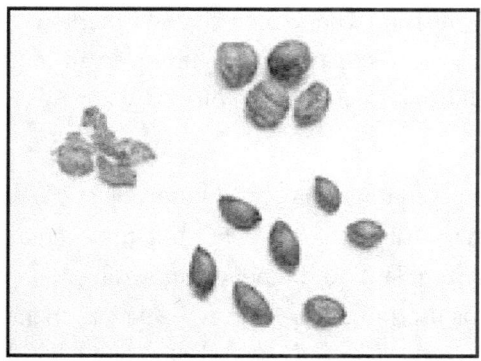

**Fig. 4.11 : Malkangani seeds**

## Extra Features

Seeds are completely enclosed in an orange red aril and are wrinkled.

## Chemical Constituents

The seeds contain nutrient rich (52%) seed oil and alkaloids have sedative and antidepressant actions such as celastrine, paniculatin among other active alkaloids. These active compounds are also being used as an antimalarial agent, and are currently used in modern medicines like Pristimerin.

## Standards of Quality

| | |
|---|---|
| Total ash | ≯ 4.0% |
| Acid insoluble ash | ≯ 1.0% |
| A.S.E. | ≮ 40.0% |
| W.S.E. | ≮ 08.0% |

## Ayurvedic Properties

| | | |
|---|---|---|
| **Rasa** | : | (taste) Katu - Pungent, Tikta - Bitter |
| **Guna** | : | quality - Teekshna - strong, piercing |
| **Vipaka** | : | It remains with pungent taste even after digestion. |
| **Veerya** | : | Hot potency. |
| **Prabhava** | : | Special medicinal effect - Medhya - improves intelligence. |

## Uses

### Pharmacological uses

Many pharmacological studies deal with its effects on the central nervous system, and the tranquilizing property of the alkaloidal fractions of the oil. The seed oil sedated rats in a dose of 1 g/kg body weight on intramuscular administration. On intraperitoneal exposure, this effect was less marked. In cats 50 - 100 mg/ kg oil proves hypertensive with a fall in cardiac output. bradycardia and marked increase in pulse pressure. The extract showed marked CNS depressing activlty (230 ± 5mg/kg body weigh. Without loss of the righting reflex even in larger doses than above. Studies have been done on the tranquillising fraction of the oil.

## Traditional Uses

For thousands of years, Ayurveda men have used the Celastrus seeds for their potent medicinal properties. It was used for many different ailments, but most notably it was administered as a powerful brain tonic, appetite stimulant, and emetic. According to Greco-Arabic Yunani medicine, the oil of the Celastrus seed was used to treat physical weakness, mental confusion, alleviate asthma symptoms, reduce headaches, cure joint pain and arthritis; and they also created a potent balm that the men believed worked as a sexual stimulant, much like modern phosphodiesterase inhibitors (i.e. sindenafil (Viagra), tadalafil (Cialis), etc.). The medicine men made a tonic of the seed oil, they used this tonic to mitigate mental fatigue, memory loss, as well as to boost memory recall, retention, and other thought processes. Traditional healers from the Chhattisgarh, Bastar region of India are known to prescribe Celastrus seeds to their patients, they recommend that anyone suffering from forgetfulness begin adding one seed to their diet daily, and then gradually increase their dosage up to 100 seeds per day. It has ability to improve mental function, memory recall and retention that has made this one of the choice herbal supplements for those working to improve dream recall, and to achieve lucid dreams.

## Therapeutic Uses

- Celastrus paniculata is a treasured medicinal herb that is revered for its effects on the brain and has been used for centuries in Ayurveda for sharpening the memory, increasing intellect, and improving concentration.

- The seed oil is used for massage with great benefit, especially in vata diseases like sciatica, lumbago, paralysis, arthritis and facial palsy.

- The seed oil is useful to hasten the healing in non-healing wounds and ulcers.

- Essential for acne, boils, eczema and hair loss.

- Excellent pain reliever.

- The oil of Malkagini is used locally in case of paralysis, facial paralysis, joint pains, sciatica, lumber pain etc.

Helpful in convulsions, migraine, loss of sleep and psychosis.

## Dosage

Seed powder: 1 - 2 g; Seed oil: 5 - 15 drops.

## Market Formulation

1. **Jyotishmati Taila :** Rasashram Pharma Pvt. Ltd. Gondal, Gujarat State.

# NEEM

## Synonyms

Margosa

## Biological Source

It consists of all aerial parts of plant *Azadiracta Indica* belonging to family *Meliaceae*.

## Geographical Source

This evergreen tree is found all over India Northern and Western parts of India with low rainfall and also other countires like Pakistan, Bangladesh. Thailand, Malaysia, Fiji and South and East Africa.

## Description of Herb

It is a large evergreen glabrous tree about 15 to 16 metres high.

**Trunk :** The trunk of the plant is tough and grows straight.

**Leaves :** Leaves are alternate, extipulate, 20 to 35 mm long, with serrated margin and are closely clustered towards the end of branches.

**Flowers :** It bears small fragrant whitish flowers in summer arranged in simple racemes.

**Fruits :** They are oval shaped berries about 1.25 to 2 cm elongated and are green in colour and turn yellow at maturity each berry bears single seed. They are bitter in taste.

**Bark :** The bark is moderately thick, rough, brown in colour. It is furrowed longitudinally and obliquely, its internal part is starchy white, laminated with characteristic smell of neem.

**Parts Used :** Flowers, leaves, bark, root bark and seeds.

## Macroscopical Characters - Leaves

| | | |
|---|---|---|
| **Colour** | : | Dark green |
| **Odour** | : | Characteristic |
| **Taste** | : | Intensely bitter |
| **Shape** | : | Leaf petioles are short, leaflets are more assymetrical and margin in dentate and euneate. |

**Fig. 4.12 : Neem Twig**

## Chemical Constituents

The leaves contain not less than 1.0 percent rutin on dry basis. Nimbin - Nimbinene, Azadiractin, Nimbondial, Nimbolide, querectin, β-sitosterol are the other constituents of neem leaves.

**Azadirachtin**

**Nimbin**

## Standards of Quality

| | | |
|---|---|---|
| FOM | ≯ | 2.0 percent |
| ASE | ≯ | 7.0 percent |
| WSE | ≯ | 19.0 percent |
| Total ash | ≯ | 12.0 percent |
| Acid insoluble ash | ≯ | 01.0 percent |

## Ayurvedic Properties

| | | |
|---|---|---|
| **Rasa** | : | Tikta, Kasaya |
| **Vipak** | : | Katu |
| **Veerya** | : | Sheeta |
| **Guna** | : | Laghu, Ruksha |
| **Doshagnata** | : | Kaphaghna, Vaatkar, Sheetveerya - pittaghana |

## Uses : Local

1. Decoction of bark and leaves is used to clean chronic and diabetic wounds.
2. In dental carries decoction is used for gargles oil is used in leprosy for external applications.

## Internal

1. It is useful in blood disorders.
2. Its decoction or swaras and leaf extract is useful in leprosy.
3. Leaf extract is used in hepatitis and anaemia.
4. Diabetic diuresis.
5. Leaf extract alongwith honey is used as good anthelmintic.
6. It is also beneficial in intermittent fevers and in malarial fever.

## Traditional Uses

Useful in blood disorders, intermittent fevers, oil is useful in leprosy, skin diseases and wounds, helpful in material fever.

## Dosage

| | | |
|---|---|---|
| Powder | : | 1 to 3 gms. |
| Leaf extract | : | 10 to 20 ml (along with honey |
| Neem oil | : | 5 to 10 drops. |

## Kalp

Nimbadechurna, Nimbaghandhak churna, Nimbaharidrakhand, Vranashodhan Taila.

## Market Formulations

1. **Neem Himalaya Capsule :** Himalaya Drug Co. Makali, Bengaluru, Karnataka.
2. **Neem MD Tablet :** Biochemix Health Care Pvt. Ltd., 7F DAV market, Yamunanagar 135001

# PASHANBHED

## Synonyms

Winter Bongonia; Silabheda.

## Biological Source

It consists of rhizomes of *Bergenia ciliate* (Haw.) Sternb., Syn. *Bergenia ligulata* (Wall.) Engl. family Saxifragaceae.

## Geographical Source

A small perennial herb commonly found in temperate Himalayas from Bhutan to Kashmir at an altitude between 2000 - 3000 m and in Khasia hills upto 1200 m altitude in Meghalaya. It is collected in Chamba, Kullu, Simla, Uttarakhand.

## Description of Herb

A perennial herb with short, thick, fleshy stems and stout thick rhizomatous root.

- Leaves are ovate or broadly ovate, with entire margin and 5 - 15 cm long. It bears trichomes on both sides.

- Flowers are white or pinkish white, 1.2 - 3 cm diameter forming cymose panicle. Fruits are sub-globose with long persistent styles and surrounded by erect calyx lobes.

- Seeds are smooth and elongated.

- Roots and rhizomes are with brown coloured cork, cylindrical shaped with the size of 1.5 - 3 cm long and 1 - 2 cm in diameter. The rhizomes show the presence of small roots, ridges furrows and root scars distinct, odour aromatic, taste astringent.

## Cultivation and Collection

Pashanbhed best grows in hot humid climate and tropical sub tropical condition. It requires red sandy loam soil with pH 5.5 – 7. The seedlings or stem cutting both preferred for propagation. The stem cuttings preferred and planted in nursery beds during May - June months. The plant will sprout out within a month. These nursery plants are suitable for planting in open field during rainy season at distance of 20 × 20 cm. Proper weeding and hoeing required at regular interval. In the initial stage of plantation it requires watering on every third day and requires fortnightly after establishment of plant.

It is auctioned from time to time by state forest corporation of Uttarakhand at Rshikesh market.

Crops are harvested by digging method in month of November/December after about 150 days of plantation. Roots are cleaned, cut into small pieces, dried and packed in polythene lined gunny bags.

## Macroscopic Characters

### Root Stalks

**Colour**     :     Yellowish brown

**Odour**      :   Characteristic aromatic and slight

**Taste**      :   Astringent

**Size**       :   4.2 - 12.3 cm long and 1.2 - 2.0 cm in diameter

**Shape**      :   Barrel shaped

**Fig. 4.13 : Pashan bhed roots**

## Extra features

**Fracture**   :   Short and fibrous

**Texture**    :   Rough

It shows presence of small rootlets, root scars and furrows. The transversely cut surface shows outer ring of brown coloured cork, short middle cortex, vascular bundles and large central pith.

## Chemical Constituents

Major phenolic compound bergenin, tannic acid, (+)-catechin, gallicin, flavonoids, benzenoids, gallic acid, lactone and glucose.

## Standards of Quality

**Foreign matter**           :   Not more than 2 per cent,

**Total Ash**                :   Not more than 13 per cent,

**Acid-insoluble ash**       :   Not more than 0.5 per cent,

**Alcohol-soluble extractive** :   Not less than 9 per cent,

**Water-soluble extractive** :   Not less than 15 per cent,

## Ayurvedic Properties

**Rasa**       :   Tikta, Kasaya

**Guna**       :   Laghu

**Veerya**     :   Sheet

**Vipaka**     :   Katu

## Pharmacological Activity

- The rhizomes posses antiurolithic property, it inhibits formation of stone, study reveals, major constituents bergenin responsible for dissolution of urinary calculi. Furthermore the diuretic activity of rhizomes contributed synergistically.

- The roots showed antidiabetic acitivity through stimulation of pancreatic islets and release of insulin similar to clinically proved sulphonylureas.

- It is one of the herb from formulae of popular hepatoprotective polyherbal formulation i.e. Liv 52. In individual preclinical studies it showed potent hepatoprotective potential.

- The roots also found to posses antipyretic, anti-inflammatory and antihypertensive property.

- In in-vitro studies, rhizome found to posses potent antioxidant and anticancer property and have prospective clinical use as precursor for preventive medicine.

## Traditional Uses

- Pashanbheda is used in Ayurveda and Unani system of medicine for treatment of many diseases especially for urinary stones.

- Externally, the paste of roots is beneficial in wounds associated with edema. Its anti-inflammatory property finds a use in the treatment of abscesses and cutaneous infections.

- The roots are rubbed down and given with honey to children when teething.

- The roots are used in treatment of vesicular calculi, urinary discharges, excessive uterine haemorrhage, diseases of the bladder, dysentery, menorrhagia, spleenic enlargement and heart diseases. Ayurveda mentions, the roots as bitter, acrid, post digestion pungent and cool in potency. Pashanbhed is tridoshnashak (balances Vata, Pitta and Kapha).

## Doses

| | | |
|---|---|---|
| **Dried powered rhizomes** | : | 1-3 gm twice a day. |
| **For decoction** | : | 20-30 gm rhizomes |

## Market Formulations

1. **Ashmarihar Kashay :** VHCA Herbals, G.T Road, Gharaunda, Karnal, Haryana.

2. **Calcure tablet :** Atreya ayurvedic pharmacy. Company, Baghpat.

3. **Nieren syrup and capsule :** Island Healthcare Private Limited, Bhiwadi, Rajasthan

# PARIJATAK

A tale is given in *Vishnu Purana* to explain its origin, "This shrub was a king's daughter, named, *Parijataka*. She fell in love with the Sun, who soon deserted her, on which she killed herself and was burnt. This shrub arose from her ashes". Hence it caste sits flowers in the morning as it cannot bear the light of Sun. The tree is sometimes called the *tree of sorrow*, because the flowers lose their brightness during daytime.

In another story, which appears in *Bhagavata Purana*, the *Mahabharata* and the *Vishnu Purana*, parijat appeared as the result of the *Samudra manthan* (Churning of the Milky Ocean) and Lord Krishna battled with Indra to win parijat. In several Hindu religious stories, is often related to the Kalpavriksha.

Besides, its fragrant flowers are esteemed as votive offerings in temples and made into garlands.

## Synonyms

Night Jasmine

## Biological Source

It consists of flowers, leaves and fruits of plant *Nyctanthes arbor-tristis* L. belonging to family Nyctaginaceae.

The scientific name arbor-tristis also means "sad tree".

## Geographical Source

It is native to southern Asia, stretching across northern Pakistan and Nepal through Northern India to Southeast Thailand. It grows at sea level and upto 1500 m altitude.

**Fig. 4.14 : Flowering parijatak herb**

## Description of Herb

It is a hardy, large shrub or a small tree upto 10 m high, with grey or greenish white rough bark and quadrangular branches.

- **Leaves** are opposite, ovate, acute, coriaceous, covered with stiff white hairs.
- **Flowers** are small in size, sweet scented, sessile, 3 - 7 together in pedunculate heads, arranged in trichotomous cymes. Flowers tubular, orange red with white limb. Anthers 2, sub-sessile, inserted near the mouth of corolla tube.
- **Fruits** are capsular, capsule upto 1 cm long, orbicular, compressed and light in weight.

## Ayurvedic Properties

| | | |
|---|---|---|
| **Rasa** | : | Tikta (bitter) |
| **Guna** | : | Laghu (light), Ruksha (dry) |
| **Veerya** | : | Ushna (heating) |
| **Vipaka** | : | Katu (pungent) |
| **Prabhava** | : | None |

## Macroscopic Characters

### Flowers

The flowers are fragrant, with a five to eight lobed white corolla with an orange red centre; they are produced in clusters of two to seven together, with individual flowers opening at dusk and finishing at dawn.

**Calyx** is 6 - 8 mm long, narrowly campanulate, hairy outside, globorous inside truncate or obscurely toothed or lobed, ciliated.

**Corolla** glaborous and is more than 13 mm long; tube is 6 - 8 mm long, orange coloured, about equaling the limbs; lobes are white and unequally obcordate and cuneate.

### Leaves

The leaves are opposite, ovate, acute or acuminate, very scabrous with unicellular warty trichomes and glandular hairs. Leaves are simple, 6 - 12 cm long and 2 - 6.5 cm broad, with an entire maring.

### Fruits

The fruit is a flat brown heart-shaped to round capsule. Two cm diameter, with two sections each containing a single seed. These are long and broad, obcordate or nearly orbicular, compressed, 2-celled.

### Seeds

Seeds are exalbuminous, testa is thick, outer layer of large transparent cells is heavily vascularised.

## Chemical Constituents

**Leaves** contain β-sitosterol, astragaline, nicotiflorin, oleanolic acid, upeol, nyctanthic acid, tannic acid, flavanol glycosides, tridoid glycosides, ascorbic acid, methyl salicylate, trace of volatile oil, carotene, friedeline and mannitol.

**Flowers** contain essential oil, nyctanthin, tannin, carotenoid, glycosides, β-monogentiobioside ester of α-crocetin (or crocin - 3), β-monogentiobioside, β-D monoglucoside ester of α-crocetin, β-digentiobioside ester of α-crocetin (or crocin - 1).

Volatile oil compositin is similar to jasmine, majorly it contains α-pinene, p-cymene, 1-hexanol methyl heptanone, phenyl acetaldehyde, 1-deconol and anisaldehyde.

**Seeds** contain arbortristoside A and B, glycerides of linoleic acid, oleic acid, lignoceric acid, stearic acid, palmitic and myristic acids, nyctanthic acid, 3 - 4 secotriterpene acid.

**Bark** contains glycosides and alkaloids.

**Stem** contains glycoside-naringenin-4-0-βglucapyranosyl-α-xylopyranoside and β-sitosterol.

## Uses

## Pharmacological Activity

**Leaves :** The leaves are reported to posses antibacterial, antifungal, anthelmintic and antioxidant potential in in-vitro studies, whiel found as anti-inflammatory, hepatoprotective, immunopotential, anti-pyretic properties in in-vitro studies.

**Flowers :** Showed diuretic, anti-bilious, antioxidant, anti-inflammatory, sedative, anti-filarial activity in various pharmacological studies.

**Seeds :** The seeds were reported to posses antibacterial, antifungal, immunomodulatory, anti-leishmanial activity.

## Traditional Uses

- **Leaves :** Bitter tonic, cholagoguc, febrifuge, anti-intiarinmatory, antispasmodic, hypotensive, respiratory stimulant. Used for fvers, rheumatism, obstinate sciaticia.

- The decoction of its leaves is taken with honey thrice a day for 3 days in intermittent fever in various parts of the country. Besides, its leaves are used as a poultice in sciatica pain, in chronic and billous fever and as a safe purgative for children.

- The bark of the tree may be used as a tanning material and leaves are sometimes, used for polishing wood and ivory. Leaves are antibilious, laxative, diaphoretic, diuretic, cholagogue, mild bitter tonic and expectorant and are useful in fevers and rheumatism. A decoction of the leaves is given in sciatica. Leaf juice mixed with little sugar is given to children as a remedy for intestinal worms. Bark is expectorant. Powdered seeds are used for curing the scurvy of scalps. (The Wealth of India, VII, 70); Chopra et al, 1956 : 177, CCRAS, 1990 : 164 - 64).

- Traditionally recommended as appetizer, anti-pyretic, anti-pruritic, relieves cough, diuretic, promotes sweating, purifies blood and as anti-pioson.

## Market Formulations

**Kamlahar Capsule :**

- **Khatore Pharmaceuticals (P) Ltd. P.O. :** Barbil, Dist. Keonjhar, Orissa - 758035.

**Sahul's Rumarid Gold Capsule :**

- **Sahul India Ltd. :** Mangalam - B, 26 Hemanta Basu Sarani, Kolkata - 700001.

# SHIWAN

## Synonyms

White teak, Gambhari, Shewan.

## Biological Source

It consists of leaves fruits and roots of plant *Gmelina arborea* Roxb and belongs to family Verbenaceae

## Geographical Source

It is common road side plant distributed throughout India in deciduous forests; in Maharashtra common in the Satpudas, Khandesh.

## Cultivation

Gmelina is reported to tolerate annual temperature of 20 to 26°C, it can favourably grow on many soils of pH of 6 to 8. It requires less irrigation, rainfall and can tolerate a 6-7 month dry season.

It can be best grown with seed propagation. Seeds, retaining their viability for only about 12 months. Soaking of seeds in water before sowing gives best results. The spacing at 5 × 5 cm is recommended. It sometimes intercropped with beans, cashew, corn, peanuts, and tobacco.

## Description of Herb

It is an un branched plant growing to maximum height of 20 m with a girth of 1.5 - 2 m. Bark is smooth, whitish gray; leaves opposite, broadly ovate, cordate, glandular. Brownish yellow flowers in terminal panicles; drup fleshy fruit of ovoid shape containing 1 to 4 seeds.

## Leaves

Leaves arc simple, pelidate exstipulate decussate opposite, more or less heart shaped, 10-25 cm long, and 5-18 cm wide.

**Fig. 4.15 : Shiwan tree**

## Flowers

The yellow or brown flowers are bisexual, bractate arranged in panicked cymes 15-30 cm long, which appears after leaf fall. The trumpet-shaped flowers are 4 cm long and hairy and short-stalked. The trumpets flare open into a gaping mouth with 5 distinct lobes.

## Fruits

Fruiting starts from May onwards up to June. The fruit is ovoid, glossy drupe 2-2.5 cm long and contains 1-4 seeds. Fruits become yellow orange on ripening and developed sweat taste.

**Fig. 4.16 : Shivan leaves**

## Bark

| | | |
|---|---|---|
| **Color** | : | Stem bark - light grey- externally; pale yellow white - internally |
| | : | Root bark - yellowish |
| **Odour** | : | Characteristic |
| **Taste** | : | Mucilaginous, sweetish with slight bitterness |
| **Size:** | | Varying |
| **Shape** | : | Thicker - arc curved and channelled Thinner ones form single quills |
| **Extra-** | : | Stem bark - exfoliated with light colored patches with lenticels |
| **feature** | : | Root bark - surface is rugged, due to the presence of vertical cracks, ridges fissures. |
| **Fracture** | : | Short and granular |
| **Roots** | : | Cylindrical with their layer of grey bark outer surface is rought due to lenti cells, central cylinder of wood is porous, hard and light |

## Chemical Constituents

The leaves of shiwan reported to have tetrahydroflavone, iridoid glycosides gmelinoside A-L, flavonoids likes luteolin, quercetin and β-sitosterol. The heart wood found to contains lignin such as gummadiol. epigummadiol gmelinol and paulownin. It also contain steroidal content such as β-sitosterol and campesterol.

The root and bark contain traces of alkaloid. Roots contains hentriacontanol-1, a sesquiterpene, ceryl alcohol, (β-sitosterol and octacosanol. Flavonoids such as luteolin and apigenin

## Standards of Quality

| | | |
|---|---|---|
| Foreign organic matter | : | Not more than 2 per cent, |
| Total Ash | : | Not more than 5 per cent, |
| Acid-insoluble ash | : | Not more than 0.3 per cent, |
| Alcohol-soluble extractive | : | Not less than 7 per cent, |
| Water-soluble extractive | : | Not less than 20 per cent, |

## Ayurvedic Description

| | | |
|---|---|---|
| **Rasa** | : | Tikta, kasaya, madhur |
| **Guna** | : | Guru |
| **Verrya** | : | Ushna |
| **Vipaka** | : | Katu |

## Uses

### Pharmacological Uses

- The methanolic extracts of stem bark of G. arborea Roxb shown to posses free radical scavenging Activity.

- The stem bark extracts of *G.arborea* showed significant antimicrobial activities against Gram positive and gram negative organism.

- The alcoholic and aqueous leaves extracts of *Gmelina arborea* Roxb exhibited anthelmintic activity at 100mg/ml concentration.

- The methanolic extract of *Gmelina arborea* shown significant diuretic activity on albino rats.

- The ethanolic extract of *G.arborea* shown potential protective effect against doxorubicin (DOX) induced cardiac toxicity by increasing cardiac markers activities in plasma.

- The ethanolic extract of *G.arborea* bark at dose of 420 mg/kg was found to reduce the increase of blood sugar in streptozotacin (50 mg/kg) induced diabetes through reinforcing the role of GSH as free radical scavenger and in the repair of free radical caused biological damage.

- The methanolic extract of *Gmelina arborea* and ethyl acetate fraction of methanolic extract have been found to increase the total WBC count, which was lowered by cyclophosphamide, a cytotoxic drug. The drug is also capable of normalising the levels of neutrophils and lymphocytes. This indicate that *G.arborea* can stimulate the bone marrow activity and it can be useful in cancer therapy also.

- The ethanolic and aqueous bark extract of G.arborea was shown to posses mild anti-inflammatory and mild analgesic property.

## Traditional Uses

- The leaves, root, root bark and flowers are used in medicine. The drupes. which are sweetish and bitter and used as an ingredient of refrigerant decoctions for fevers and bilious affections.

- Shiwan leaves are demulcent. A paste of the leaves is robbed on the head for the relief of pain.

- The root is bitter tonic, stomachic, laxative, and galactagogue. The root is an ingredient of the Ayurvedic preparation *dasanuda*.

- The bark is a bitter tonic and stomachic, and is considered useful in fever and indigestion.

- Useful in prevention of abortions in the early stage of pregnancy, where bark powder and black gingally seeds, *manjista* and *salavari* is advised to take with milk.

## Doses

20-30 g of the drug for decoction.

## Market Formulations

1. **Dashmularishta :** General weakness (Dabur, Gaziabad, Uttar Pradesh)
2. **Arbindasava :** Tonic, in rickets fever, cough (Shree Baidyanath Ayurved Bhawan Pvt. Ltd. Gupta Lane, Kolkata.
3. **Mahavajrak Tel :** Nisha Herbals, Near Sangam Cinema, Nagpur.

# VAJRADANTI

## Synonyms

Yellow Nail dye plant

## Biological Source

It consists of dried whole plant of *Barleria prionitis* Linn family : Acanthaceae

## Geographical Source

It is found throughout the hotter parts of India.

## Cultivation

It is commonly grown as an ornamental plant in gardens.

The shrubs prefer a sunny situation on wide variety of well-drained moist soil. They tolerate temperatures only above at least 1°C. It best grows with average annual rainfall between 750 - 900 mm. The seeds are very light in weight containing 33,000 seeds/kg. Seedlings grow slowly at first i.e. germinated between 13 and 77 days following sowing. However, an established plant grows fast. These shrubs flower from September to December and fruit from January to April.and can be harvested for four years. Natural regeneration generally occurs within 1 or 2 m of the parent plant.

## Description of Herb

It is evergreen, is a tender, erect, branching, evergreen shrub bushy shrub grows up to 1 - 2 m with spiny stem nodes, elliptic to oblong, mid-green leaves, 6 to 12 centimeters long, narrowed, and pointed at both ends. Flowers are yellow and axillary, with the upper ones in spikes. Bracts and calyx are green, with the outer bract usually foliaceous. Corolla is about 4 centimeters long, flowers in summer.

**The stems** are terete, glabrous, much branched with cylindrical and tapering branchlet.

**Leaves** are smooth, opposite, ovate-elliptic to obovate, acuminate, tapering to base, entire, margin finely ciliate, bristle-tipped and about 6-15 cm long and 4-6 cm wide. The petioles are about 0.5-3 cm long, widely spreading spines present in axils.

**The flowers** are sessile, yellow in colour and often solitary in lower axils and spictate in the upper axils. Bracts are acute, linear-lanceolate, foliaceous, about 1-1.5 cm long and 0.2-0.8 cm wide with bristle tipped. The corolla is bright, golden yellow in colour with pubescent outside and glabrous inside and about 1.5 cm long. The filaments are hairy and about 2-2.5 cm long, yellowish in colour with 3mm long yellow anthers. The ovary is ovoid and sigma is long, linear, sticky and pinkish in colour.

**The fruit** is ovoid capsule containing 2 seeds. It is about 1.5-2 cm long and 0.6 - 0.8 cm wide. The seeds are oval-oblong, covered with silky copper-brown appressed hairs and measuring about 7.4-8.5 × 6-6.8 mm.

**Roots** are central tap type, with lateral roots branching in all directions.

## Macroscopic Characters

| | | |
|---|---|---|
| **Colour** | : | Vadjradanti is pale green to greenish |
| **Odour** | : | Characteristic slight |
| **Taste** | : | Bitter |
| **Extra features** | : | Crumbled pieces or coarse powder, brittle in nature. |

**Fig. 4.17 : Vajradanti herb**

## Chemical Constituents

*B. prionitis* shows presence of glycosides, saponins, flavonoids, steroids and tannins

- Glycosides like prioniside A, prioniside B, barlerinoside, verbascoside, shanzhiside methyl ester

- Saponins - lupulinoside, luteolin-7-O-β-D-glucoside

- Flavonoids - apigenin 7-0-glucoside, 6-hydroxyflavones

- Phenolic acid - *melilotic acid*, syringic acid, vanillic acid, p-hydroxybenzoic acid

It also sowed the presence of triterpenoids and steroids such as lupeol and B-sitosterol. Bark consist of 16% tannins and ellagic acid.

**Prioniside**

## Standards of Quality

| | |
|---|---|
| Foreign organic matter | Not more than 2 percent |
| Total ash | Not more than 7 percent |
| Acid-insoluble ash | Not more than 1 percent |
| Alcohol-soluble extractive | Not less than 4 percent |
| Water-soluble extractive | Not less than 10 percent |

## Ayurvedic Properties

| | | |
|---|---|---|
| **Rasa** | : | Madhura, Tikta |
| **Guna** | : | Snigdha |
| **Virya** | : | Usna |
| **Vipaka** | : | Katu |

## Therapeutic Uses

Charaka recommended leaf paste as an ingredient of hot poultices and steam bath in the treatment of stiffness of limbs, enlargement of scrotum, sciatica and erysipelas.

Sushruta prescribed flowers internally in migraine, internal abscesses, oedema, haemoptysis, urethral discharges, seminal disorders and also to reduce obesity.

The herb's extract in oil was prescribed for massage in arthritis and gout.

Traditionally the plant parts have been recommended in different health aliments.

## Traditional Uses

Astringent and recommended to strengthen the gums, also prescribed in diarrhoea.

## Leaves

- Fresh leaf juice used to control diarrhoea, urinary infection
- The crushed leaves were applied on wounds and boils
- The leaves were applied locally for joint pain and swelling.
- Fresh leaf juice applied on the scalp in fungal infection, furthermore it promotes hair growth
- Leaves and flowering tops are recommended as diuretics and in urinary infection

## Fruit

Fruits are bitter, acrid, anthelmintic, haemolytic; also prescribed in gingivitis as expectorant.

## Seeds

Seed powder were used as emetic and expectorant.

## Bark

Bark as astringent, useful in diarrhea whooping cough and expectorant.

## Roots

Roots are utilized in bleeding gums, loose teeth, dental cavities and sensitive teeth.

Decoction of Barleria prionitis root for treatment of viral fevers.

The Ayurvedic pharmacopoeia of India recommended it in goiter and psychological disorder.

The whole plant is antiseptic, diuretic and applied over boils and glandular swelling.

## Pharmacological Uses

- It exhibited following pharmacological effects as
- Antimicrobial activity over a wide pathological microorganism.
- Iridoid glycoside shown to have potent antiviral property
- Whole plant extracts posses anthelmintic activity in vitro studies.
- The Iridoid glycoside present in roots shown reduced spermatogenesis in male albino rats
- The areal parts of plant shown to posses strong antioxidant hepatoprotective, antidiabetic and cytoprotective ability in experimental animals
- The plant also exhibited strong anti-inflammatory, anti-arthritic, analgesic and diuretic property

## Marketed Formulations

1. **Vicco Vajradanti Tooth Powder and Tooth Paste :** Vicco Laboratories, Near Tata Cancer Hospital, Bhoiwada, Mumbai - 400002.

2. **Sahacharadi Taila :** Gururaja Ayurvedic Pharma Visveshwara Nagar, Mysore, Karnataka.

✍ ✍ ✍

# BIBLIOGRAPHY

1. Herbal Drugs in Indian Pharmaceutical Industry, 1979 S. L. Kapoor, R. Mitra. Economic Botany Information Service, National Botanical Research Institute, LUCKNOW 226601.

2. CRC Hand book of Ayurvedic Medicinal plants, L. D. Kapoor, Taylor and Francis, CRC Press USA.

3. Text book of Pharmacognosy, Second Edition, 2012, M. K. Gupta, P. K. Sharma, Pragati Prakashan, Pragati Bhavan, 240 W. K. Raod, Meerat, 250 001.

4. Pharmacognosy IV, V, VI, VII, 2013, S. B. Gokhale, A. P. Purohit, C. K. Kokate, Nirali Prakashan, Abhyudaya Pragati, 1312, Shivaji Nagar, Off J. M. Road, Pune, 411005.

5. CRC Handbook of Ayurvedic Medicinal Plants, L. D. Kapoor, Taylor and Francis, CRC Press, USA.

6. Indian Pharmacopocia Vol. I - IV, 6th Edition, 1996, Ministry of Health, Govt. of India, New Delhi.

7. Pharmacognosy, C. K. Kokate, A. P. Purohit, S. B. Gokhale, 48th Edition, 2012, Nirali Prakashan, Pune 5.

8. Pharmacognosy Phytochemistry of medicinal plants, Jean Bruneton, 2nd Edition, 1999. Intercept Ltd. London.

9. Pharmacognosy, Trease GE and Evans W. C. 12th Edition 1983, Bailliere Tindall U. K.

10. Pharmacognosy, Tyler E. E. Brady Lyn R and Robbers J. E. Ninth edition, 1988 Burger, Minneaopolis, Minnesota. U.S.A.

11. Text book of Pharmacognosy, Wallis T.E., 5th Edition 1967, J & A Churchill Ltd. London (U.K.)

12. Medicinal Plants of India Vol. I, 1976, ICMR, New Delhi.

13. Glossary of Indian Medicinal Plants, Chopra R. N., Chopra, J. C. and Nayar S. I., 1956, CSIR, New Delhi.

14. Wealth of India – Raw Material Series, 1948-1976, Council of Scientific and Industrial Research, New Delhi.

15. Indian Materia-Medica Vol. I & II, Third Edition, reprint 2009, Popular Prakashan, Mahalaxmi, Mumbai 26.

16. Herbal drugs in Indian Pharamaceutical Industry, 1979, S. L. Kapoor and R. Mitra, Economic Botany Information Service, National Botanical Research Institute, Lucknow 226601.

✐ ✐ ✐

# GLOSSARY

Most of the technical terms used for the macroscopic and microscopic descriptions of crude drugs and also to describe their pharmacological and pharmaceutical uses are included in this glossary.

## 1. BOTANICAL TERMS

| | | |
|---|---|---|
| Achene | : | A simple dry one-seeded, ndehiscent fruit with unfused seed coat and fruit wall, but with no special method to liberate the seeds. |
| Adventitious | : | Arising from abnormal position. |
| Adventitious roots | : | Arising from stems or leaf cutting but not from primary root. |
| Adventitious buds | : | A bud which develops in some other place than the axils of leaves or stem apices. |
| Aerenchyma | : | Tissue comprising of thin walled cells with large airsacs found in different parts of plants. |
| Aleurone grains | : | Protein granules found in plants, quite often in seeds. |
| Algae | : | Simple lower plants capable of carrying out the photosynthesis and with unicellular organs or reproduction. |
| Androecium | : | Collective term, for the stamens of flower. |
| Angiosperm | : | Flowering plant. |
| Anther | : | Pollen bearing part of a stamen. |
| Anticlinal | : | Situated approximately at right angles to outer surface of plant part. |
| Annual | : | Plant that completes its life cycle from seed germination on seed production followed by death, in a single season. |
| Annual ring | : | The layer of xylem (wood) formed by one year's growth of cambium. |
| Annual thickening | : | Internal thickening of wall of xylem vessel so as to form rings at intervals alongwith its length. |
| Apical | : | Of the tip. |
| Apothecium | : | Cup-shaped fruit body of certain ascomycete fungi. |
| Aril (Arillus) | : | Succulent development of stalk or base of seeds of fungi (mycophyta). |
| Ascomycetes | : | Group of fungi (mycophyta). |
| Ascospore | : | A spore produced by sac (ascomycete). |
| Ascus | : | A sac-like structure within which ascospores are produced. |
| Auxins | : | Growth regulating substance or plant hormones. |

| Awn | : | Siff bristle-like appendage occurring frequently on the flowering glumes of grasses or on seeds. |
| Axil | : | The upper angle between a twig or leaf stalk and the axis from which it grows. |
| Bud | : | Terminal structure consisting of meristemic tissue, covered wholly or in part by overlapping leaves. |
| Cambium | : | Layer or meristematic cells between xylem and phloem tissues. |
| Carpel | : | A female floral organ which bears and encloses ovules. |
| Chitin | : | Nitrogen containing polysaccharide derivative found in insects and lower plants. |
| Conidiospore | : | A sexual spore of certain fungi cut off externally at apex of specialized hypha. |
| Conidium | : | A hypha which produces conidia. |
| Cork | : | Suberized tissue formed from the cork cambium on stem and root surfaces of dicot plants. |
| Corm | : | A short, often globose, upright, underground stem which stores food; differs from a bulb in that the latter consists chiefly of fleshy storage leaves growing from a small stem, whereas a corm is chiefly stem tissue. |
| Cortex | : | Tissues lying between the epidermis and endodermis of a stem or root. |
| Cotyledon | : | A food-digesting and food-storing part of an embryo; also known as seed-leaf. |
| Cuticle | : | Waxy layer formed on outer walls of epidermal cells. |
| Cutin | : | Waxy substance containing cutinogenic acids impermeable to water; the cuticle is composed of cutin. |
| Drupe | : | A simple fleshy fruit in which the endocarp (inner wall of ovary) becomes hard and stony, and encloses one or two seeds. |
| Emergence | : | An outgrowth, consisting of epidermal and cortical tissues and lacking vascular tissues, e.g. rose prickles. |
| Endodermis | : | The surface layer of cell in leaves and other soft plant parts. |
| Fibre | : | An elongated, tapering thick-walled strengthening cell occurring in various plant parts. |
| Fossil | : | An impression or trace of a plant or plant part in the earth's crust. |
| Guard cells | : | Paired epidermal, chlorophyllous cell which enclose stoma. |
| Hilum | : | Scar on a seed coat, making the place of an attachment of the seed stalk to the seed. |

| | | |
|---|---|---|
| Hydathode | : | Water excreting gland occurring on the edges or tips of leaves of many plants. |
| Hypha | : | A fungal filament. |
| Inner bark | : | The phloem and cortex of bark. |
| Integument | : | The coat of an ovule. |
| Inulin | : | Insoluble polysaccharide or vegetable origin. |
| Isobilateral | : | A structure of which both sides get equally exposed and possesses same structure on both sides. |
| Latex | : | A characteristic milky fluid produced by various flowering plants, which oozes out from cut surface and rapidly coagulates on exposure to air. It contains a number of chemicals like sugars, oil, enzyme, alkaloids, etc. e.g. fig, banyan, papaya, popy capsules. |
| Lenticel | : | In woody stems and other plant parts, a pore through which exchange of gases occurs; in woody stems, lenticells occur in bark. |
| Lichen | : | Dual organism formed from symbiotic association of two plants, a fungus and an algae. |
| Lignin | : | A complex aromatic compound deposited in cell walls of sclerenchyma, xylem vessels, tracheids, making them strong and rigid. |
| Mericarp | : | One seeded portion of schizocarp. |
| Micropyle | : | The minute opening in the integument of an ovule or seeds, through which a pollen tube grows to reach the female gametophyte. |
| Nucleolus | : | A small particle containing RNA, in nucleus. |
| Outer bark | : | The cork and cork cambium tissue of woody stem and root. |
| Pathogen | : | Disease producing parasite. |
| Pericycle | : | A layer between endodermis and conducting tissue. |
| Perithecium | : | A globose or pear-shaped ascocarp with a small, definite pore. |
| Phelloderm | : | Secondary tissue formed by cork cambium. |
| Polyploid | : | Having more than two sets of chromosomes. |
| Radicle | : | The lower portion of the hypocotyl which grows into the primary root of a seedling. |
| Raphides | : | Needle-like crystals of calcium oxalate occurring in bundles. |
| Runner | : | A stem which grows horizontally over the surface of the soil, often developing new plants at its nodes; also horizontal, surface hyphae of certain fungi (e.g. Rhizopus). |

| | | |
|---|---|---|
| Schizocarp | : | Dry fruit formed from a syncarpous ovary that splits at maturity into its individual carpels forming one seeded fruits known as mericarps. |
| Sclerenchyma | : | A strengthening tissue composed of thick walled, elongated cells (fibres) or shorter cells (stone cells). |
| Stele | : | Vascular tissue, immediately lying internally to the endodermis which contains xylem, phloem, pericycle, and sometimes, pith and medullary rays. Detailed structure of stele may vary from plant to plant. |
| Suberin | : | Thick-walled mixture of oxidation and condensation products of various fatty acids. Suberin is present generally in cork cells making them impervious to water. |
| Tracheid | : | A type of non-perforate conducting and strengthening cell in xylem tissue, or elongated tapering form with pitted walls. |
| Turgidity | : | State of being plump or swollen as a result of internal water pressure. |

## 2. PHARMACOLOGICAL TERMS

| | | |
|---|---|---|
| Abortifacient | : | An agent which causes an abortion. |
| Addiction | : | To form a habit or enslavement to some habit. Examples : opium, cannabis (ganja). |
| Amenorrhoea | : | A term used to indicate the absence or suppression of menstruation. |
| Adjuvant | : | One which assists. |
| Antagonistic | : | One which opposes the action of another. |
| Analgesic | : | Substance which relieves pain by acting on central nervous system. They are of two types : |
| | | (a) Narcotic analgesics : opium, Indian hemp |
| | | (b) Antipyretic analgesics : aconite |
| Anaesthetic | : | Drugs which cause insensibility to touch or pain, may be general or local. |
| Anodyne | : | An agent which relieves pain, but is milder than analgesic e.g. belladonna. |
| Anthelmintic | : | Substance used to expel the worms out of intestine like thread worm, tape worm, round worm etc. They do not kill the worms essentially, e.g. santonin quassia. |
| Antidote | : | Substance which neutralises the poisons or their ill effects. |
| Antidiaphoretic | : | Substance reducing the profuse sweating, e.g. belladonna, hyocyamus. |
| Antiemetic | : | A drug that prevents vomiting. |
| Antifebrile | : | Substance reducing fever e.g. quinine. |

| Antiphlogistic | : | External application employed to reduce inflammation, e.g. aconite. |
| Antiprotozoal | : | Against Protozoa (e.g. unicellular micro-organisms) e.g. kurchi. |
| Antiseptic | : | Substance used to check the growth or development of micro-oganisms. |
| Antisialagogue | : | A compound that reduces or lessens the secretion, of saliva e.g. belladonna. |
| Antispasmodic | : | Substances which relieve or control spasms (pain) of voluntary or involuntary muscles, e.g datura, valerian, lobelia, asafoetida, opium, belladonna. |
| Aphrodisiac | : | An agent stimulating the sexual desire. |
| Aperient | : | Mild laxative e.g. rhubarb, isapgol. |
| Appetizer | : | Compound that stimulates the desire for food. |
| Arthritis | : | Inflammation of a joint. |
| Articular | : | Relating to a joint. |
| Antidiarrhoeals | : | Rapid passage of faecal matter through gastrointestinal tract and frequently passage of liquid faeces. |
| Aromatic | : | Substance having fragrant agreeable odour, e.g. cardamom clove, cinnamom, nutmeg, orange peel etc. |
| Arrhythmia | : | Loss of regularity, especially of heart. |
| Astringent | : | Precipitates proteins and causes contraction of tissues e.g. tannic acid, catechu, myrobalan. |
| Atony | : | Lack of tension, relaxation. |
| Bitter | : | Substances characterized by bitter taste, e.g. gentian, nux-vomica, cinchona etc. |
| Bradycardia | : | Slowness of heart beat. |
| Bronchitis | : | Inflammation of bronchial mucous membrane. |
| Carminative | : | A substance that removes gases from the G.I. tract, e.g. cardamom, peppermint, asafoetida. |
| Cathartic | : | Active purgative usually producing severe evacuation, may or may not be accompanied with pain, e.g. jalap, cotocynth, castor oil, aloe, rhubarb. |
| Chronic | : | Of long duration. |
| Colic | : | Spasmodic pains in the abdomen. |
| Colitis | : | Inflammation of the colon. |
| Convulsion | : | A violent spasm. |

| | | |
|---|---|---|
| Counter-irritant | : | Substances producing superficial and artificial inflammation in order to exercise a good effect on the part applied e.g. camphor, turpentine oil. |
| Demulcent | : | Midicament that soothes or protects the mucous membrane or any other part to which it is applied. |
| Deodorant | : | An agent which neutralises, removes or destroys foul odour. |
| Depressant | : | Drugs which lower functional activities or retard the physiological action of an organ, e.g. opium. |
| Diorrhoea | : | Frequent discharge of more or less fluid fecal matter from bowel. |
| Diaphoretic | : | An agent which increases perspiration or sweating e.g. camphor, opium. |
| Digestive | : | Drugs which assist the stomach and intestine in their normal function of promoting the digestion of foods, e.g. capsicum, papain. |
| Diuretic | : | Drugs which increase the flow or secretion of urine or increase the quantity of urine, e.g. buchu, caffeine |
| Emetics | : | Substances which induce or produce vomitting e.g. ipcacuanha, mustard, senega. |
| Emmenagogues | : | Substances which stimulate the menstrual flow. |
| Emollient | : | An agent that softens and smoothens the part when applied locally, e.g. honey, linseed, liquid paraffin and lard. |
| Euphoria | : | A feeling of well being. |
| Excitant | : | An agent that stimulates the special function of the body according to the action, as motor, cerebral, etc. e.g. balsam of tolu, glycyrrhiza, senega. |
| Febrifuge | : | An agent that lessens fever, i.e. antipyretic. |
| Flatulence | : | Gas in the digestive tract due to fermentation or decomposition. |
| Haemorrhage | : | Bleeding. |
| Haemostatics | : | An agent that arrests bleeding. |
| Hydrogogue | : | Drug promoting watery evacuation of the bowel e.g. calomel, jalap. |
| Hypnotics | : | Drugs that induce sleep without cerebral excitement, e.g. hops, opium. |
| Insomnia | : | Sleeplessness. |
| Irritant | : | An agent which, when used locally, produces more or less inflammation, e.g. cantharides. |
| Labour | : | Child birth, delivery. |
| Laxative | : | Drugs that loosen the bowels, mild purgative, e.g senna. |
| Mydriatics | : | Remedy causing dialation of the pupil and paralysis of ciliary muscles, e.g. belladonna, datura. |

| | | |
|---|---|---|
| Narcotic | : | Substance that produces stupor or sleep, e.g. Indian hemp, opium. |
| Nasal | : | Related to nose. |
| Nauseant | : | Causing inclination to vomit. |
| Oxytocic | : | An agent that causes expulsion of the contents of uterus by contracting the uterine muscles. |
| Purgative | : | An agent that causes evacuation of bowels, e.g. senna, jalap, colocynth, rhubarb, aloe. |
| Refrigerant | : | An agent that relieves thirst and is cooling, e.g. orange tamarind. |
| Rubefacient | : | Agent which reddens the skin producing a local congestion, dilating the vessels and thus, resulting in the increased blood supply, e.g. oil of turpentine, capsicum, mustard, flax seed. |
| Sedative | : | Agent which lowers the functional activities, or substances which quiet the nervous system. |
| Spasms | : | Involuntary muscular contractions. |
| Stimulants | : | Agents which temporally increase the functional activity, classified according to the organ upon which they act as : cardiac, bronchial, gastric, cerebral, intestinal, nervous, motor, vasomotor and respiratory, e.g. camphor, turpentine, strychnine, caffeine, ephedrine asafoetida. |
| Stomachic | : | Substances increasing the secretion of gastric juice and also the functional activity of the stomach, e.g. dill, fennel, coriander, gentian. |
| Styptic | : | Anything that checks the haemorrhage, e.g. tannic acid |
| Tachycardia | : | Rapid beating of the heart. |
| Tumour | : | Swelling or abnormal growth of tissue. |
| Ulcer | : | A lesion on the surface of the skin or mucous membrane. |
| Vesicant | : | An agent that produces blisters, e.g. mustard gas, cantharides. |
| Vasoconstrictor | : | Causing constriction of blood vessels. |
| Vasodilator | : | Causing dilatation or relaxation of blood vessels. |

## 3. PHARMACEUTICAL TERMS

| | | |
|---|---|---|
| Antioxidants | : | These are the agents which are used to prevent the oxidation of pharmaceutical products and their subsequent spoilage, e.g. benzoin. |
| Binding agents | : | The agents added to prevent the formation of friable granules in the manufacture of compressed tablets They are also used in the manufacture of pills e.g. mucilage of acacia, starch, gelatin solution. |
| Colouring agents | : | Substances used for the purpose of imparting colour, like chlorophyll, indigo, β-carotene, alizarin, cochireal etc. |

Diluents : The chemically and physiologically inert substances added to pharmaceutical formulations to adjust their strength or weight, e.g. starch, kaolin.

Disintegrating agents : Substances which swell rapidly when come in contact with water and help the breaking of compressed tablet in G.I. tract e.g. alginate, agar, gelatin, starch.

Dispersing agents : The substances added to suspended medium to promote and maintain the separation of the individual extremely fine particles of solid or liquid which are usually of colloidal size, e.g. sodium alginate, tragacanth.

Emulsifying agents : Emulgents, e.g. Indian gum, guar gum, tragacanth.

Flavouring agents : Substances used to mask the nauseating odour, unpleasant taste and odour of the medicines, e.g. balsam of tolu, lemon oil, orange oil, peppermint oil.

Ointments : Semi-solid, anhydrous preparations of fairly firm consistency usually with greasy (oily) water insoluble base. These constitute oils, fats, waxes or mixtures of paraffins e.g. bees wax, soft and hard paraffin.

Preservatives : Substances with antimicrobial properties used to prevent the deterioration by bacterial or fungal growth.

Suspending agents : Substances which keep the insoluble material in a finely divided form in liquid medium e.g. gum acacia, guargum, methyl cellulose.

Suppositories : Solid preparations to be inserted into rectum. These are prepared with fatty bases such as theobroma or hydrogenated fat or water soluble base, e.g. glycerine, gelatin.

Sweetening agents : Substances used to mask the bitter, nauseating or unpleasant taste of medicaments, e.g. honey, syrup, glycyrrhiza, stavia.

Thickening agents : Substances used to increase the viscosity of the preparation so as to have better mouth feel and also to have increased physical stability of suspensions or emulsions, e.g. tragacanth, starch, sodium alginate, agar.

☞ ☞ ☞

# VERNACULAR NAMES IN VARIOUS LANGUAGES OF TRADITIONAL DRUGS

## Key to Abbreviations Used

| | | | |
|---|---|---|---|
| A. Arabic | B. Bengali; | En. English; | Fr. French; | G. Gujrati; |
| Gr. German; | H. Hindi; | K. Kannada; | M. Malayalam; | Mr. Marathi; |
| Or. Oriyan; | P. Punjabi; | S. Sanskrit; | Tm. Tamil; | T. Telugu. |
| Tr. Turkish | | | | |

## TERPENOIDAL DRUGS

### Anantmula

B. Anantmul
G. Durivel
H. Salsa, Anatmul
K. Sogdeberingida
M. Nannari
Mr. Anantmul
S. Nagajihya
Tm. Nannari
T. Muttavapulagamu

### Chandan

B. Chandan
G. Chandan
H. Safedchandan
K. Chandana
M. Chandnam
Mr. Chandan
Tm. Ingam
T. Chandunamu

### Guggul

B. Guggul
G. Guggul
H. Guggul
M. Guggul
Mr. Guggul
S. Guggulu
Tm. Gukkulu
Gr. Indisches bdelliumbaum

Fr. Bdellium de'lrde
It. bdellio

### Haridra

B. Haritaki
G. Hirdo
H. Harana
K. Alate, Harade
Tm. Divya
Mr. Hirda
S. Haritaki
Tm. Kadukkai
T. Karitaki
P. Har
Or. Haridra
Gr. Mirobalanenbaum
Fr. Myrobalan belleric
It. Mirobalano

### Jatamansi

B. Jatamanshi
G. Jatamasi
H. Jatamanshi
M. Jetamanshi
Mr. Batacharea
S. Jatamanshi
Tm. Jalamansi
T. Jatamansi
Gr. Indischenarde
Fr. Nardindien
It. Spignardi

### Lasuna

B. Lasun
G. Lasun
H. Lasan
K. Bellulli
M. Velluli
Mr. Lasun
S. Ugragandha
Tm. Karuvelum
T. Nellatumma
P. Thom
Or. Rasun
Gr. Knoblauch
Fr. Ail
It. Aglio

### Maricha

B. Golmorich
G. Golmirch
M. Kurumuaka
Mr. Kalimiree
S. Milagu
Tm. Marichamu
T. Maricha
P. Golmirichi
Gr. Schwarzer pfeffer
Fr. Poivrenoir
It. Pepenero

## Nagarmotha

En. Nut-grass
S. Mustaka
H. Korehijar
B. Moothoo
Mr. Nagarmotha
Tm. Korai
K. Tungar gadoo
T. Tungamuste
M. Bimbal

## Nirgundi

S. Nirgundi
B. Nirgundi
H. Nirgandi
Mr. Nirgundi
M. Vennochi
Tm. Vennochi
T. Nallavavili
K. Niragundi

## Pippali

B. Pepul
H. Pipal
M. Pippali
Mr. Lendipimpali
S. Pipali
Tm. Thippilli
T. Pippallu

## Sallaki

S. Sallaki
En. Indian olibanum tree
B. Salai
G. Mukul salai
H. Salai, Kundur
K. Madi, Guggula
M. Kunturukkam
Mr. Salai Sallaki guggul
Tm. parangisambrani
T. Parangisambrani

## Sunthi

B. Ada
G. Adu
H. Adrak
K. Shunti
M. Inchi
Mr. Ale
S. Adrakam
Tm. Sukka
T. Sonti
Or. Ada
Gr. Ingiver
Fr. Gingembre
It. Zenzero

## Tamal Patra

S. Tamalaka
H. Tejput, Tejpatta
B. Tejput
G. Tejpat
Mr. Tamalpatra
Tm. Talishapattiri
T. Talispatri
M. Masala aku

## Tulasi

B. Tulsi
G. Tulsi
H. Tulsi
K. Vishnu-tulsi
M. Trittaru
Mr. Tulsi
S. Manjiri
Tm. Thulasi
T. Thulasi

## Vacha

Ar. Wagg-Ul-el wagg
B. Bach
En. Sweet flag
Fr. Acoreodorant
Gr. Echter kalmus
G. Vekhand

H. Bach
It. Acoroaromat
K. Baje gida
M. Vasambu
Mr. Vekhand
P. Bariboj
S. Vacha
Tm. Vasampu
T. Vasa
Tr. Egir out

## Vidanga

B. Vidang
G. Vavding
H. Vayavidang
K. Vayuvilanga
M. Vizalari
Mr. Vavding
Tm. Vayuvidangam
T. Vayuvidangam

## LIPIDS

## Bhilama

En. Marking nut
S. Bhollataka
B. Bhelu
Mr. Bibba
H. Bhilama
M. Temprakku
Tm. Serangottai
T. Bhallatamu
K. Gerkavi
G. Bhilamu

## Castor Oil

B. Bherenda
G. Divel
H. Erand
K. Harelenne
M. Amanakku
Mr. Erand tel
S. Erandi

Tm. Amanakkuchei

T.   Arnudamu

P.   Rendi

Or.  Jada

Gr.  Echter wunderbaun

Fr.  Palma christi

It.  Risino

## Karanja Oil

B.   Dahar kananja

H.   Kuranj, kiramal

K.   Karinje-kraaku

M.   purgammaram

Mr.  Karanj, kidumar

S.   karanja, Nalatarnala

Tm.  Punyamuranam

T.   kamuga-chetter

P.   Karanj

Or.  Koranjo

Gr.  Mondbohne

Fr.  Arbe de' pongolote

## Linseed

B.   Masina

G.   Alasi

H.   Alasi

K.   Agashi

M.   Cerucannam vithu

Mr.  Javas

S.   Agasi bija

T.   Arish vettu

Gr.  Echterlein

Fr.  Lincommun

It.  Linousuale

## Sesame Oil

B.   Til

G.   Til

H.   Til

K.   Achchellu

M.   Ellu

Mr.  Til

S.   Tila

Tm.  Ellu

T.   Nurrullu

## Beeswax

En.  Yellow bees wax

S.   Madhujan

B.   Mom

H.   Mom

Mr.  Men

G.   Min

M.   Mezhuku

Tm.  Mellugu

T.   Mainam

## CARBOHYDRATES
## Isapgol

B.   Eshopgol

G.   Isafaghol

H.   Isabghul

K.   Issagolu

M.   Karkalasaringi

Mr.  Isabgol

S.   Shigdhajiraka

Tm.  Ishappukol

T.   Isapagola

Gr.  Sogelwegerich

Fr.  Ispaghula

## Madhu (Mel)

B.   Madh

G.   Madh

H.   Madhu

K.   Jenu Tuppa

M.   Ten

Mr.  Madh

S.   Madhu

Tm.  Ten

T.   Tene

## MIXED CHEMICAL CONSTITUENTS
## Artemisia

G.   Chhuvaria ajmoda

H.   Kirmala

Mr.  Kirmani ova

S.   Chauhara

K.   Murni

Gr.  Strand deifuss

Fr.  Armonoise

It.  Assenzio

## Benafsha

En.  Wild violet

B.   Banosa

H.   Banaphsha

M.   Vayilettu

Mr.  Banafshah

S.   Banaphsha

Tm.  Nilapuspha

## Chitrak

B.   Chita

H.   Chitra

E.   White lead wart

G.   Chitrak

K.   Chappyiju

M.   Vellakotuveri

Mr.  Chitrak

P.   Chitrak

T.   Kodiveli

Tm.  Sitiragam

U.   Chita

## Colocynth

B.   Indrayan, makhal

G.   Indrayan, makhal

H.   Indrayan, makhal

K.   Karandali

M.   Vaikummatti, katuvelleki

Mr.  Indrayan, makhal

S.   Indrauanuni, Uirhala

Tm. Paedikani, Attutunnatti
T.    Eti-puchcha. chittipapara
P.    Kaud tumbha
Or. Kalara
Gr. Bitter zitrutte
Fr.    Coloquinte
It.     Coloquinda

## Dhataki Pushpa

S.    Dhataki
B.    Dhai
G.    Dhavdi
H.    Dhavi
K.    Bela
M.    Tatire
Mr. Dhayati
P.    Dhaur
T.     Dhataki
Tm. Velakhai

## Kalijiri

S.    Krishnajiraka
B.    Kalijira
H.    Kalongi
G.    Kaligiri
M.    Karunshiragam
Mr. Kalejire
Tm. Karunjiragam
U.    Gandana

## Kushta

B.    Kur
G.    Kut
K.    Koshtha
H.    Kut, Pachak
M.    Sepuddy
Mr. Ooplet
S.    Kushtha
Tm. Koshtam
T.     Koshtum
En. Kuth

## Malkangani

S.    Jotishmati
B.    Latafatki
E.    Staff tree
G.    Malkangani
H.    Malkanguni
M.    Palulavum
Mr. Kanguni
Tm. Vahizhurai
U.    Malkangum

## Neem

B.    Nim
H.    Nim
M.    Vepa
Mr. Kadulimb
S.    Nimba
Tm. Vepa
T.     Vepa
P.    Bakam

Or. Nimba
Gr. Margosa geneiner
Fr.    Azadarachte

## Pashanbhed

S.    Pashanabheda
H.    Pakhanbhed
Mr. Pashanbhed
B.    Patharchuri

## Parijatak

En. Night jasmine
B.    Harsinghar
Mr. Parijatak
H.    Harsinghar
M.    Mannapu
Tm. Paula malligai
T.     Sepali
K.    Parajata
G.    Jayparvati

## Vajradanti

S.    Karunta
H.    Katsareya
B.    Kantajati
Mr. Vajradanti
M.    Shemmuli
Tm. Shemmuli
T.     Mullugoranta

# BIOLOGICAL INDEX

- Acorus calamus — 1.41
- Allium sativum — 1.18
- Apis dorsata — 2.18, 3.4
- Apis mellifica — 2.18, 3.4
- Artemisia annua — 4.1
- Azadirecta indica — 4.22
- Balasamodend mukul — 1.7
- Barleria prionitis — 4.33
- Bergenia legulata — 4.24
- Bergenica ciliate — 4.24
- Boswellia serata — 1.31
- Celastrus particulars — 4.19
- Centratherum anthelminticum — 4.14
- Cinamomum tamala — 1.37
- Citrullus colocynthus — 4.10
- Commiphora abyssinia — 1.7
- Commiphora mukul — 1.7
- Curcuma longa — 1.1
- Cyperous rotendus — 1.24
- Embelia ribes — 1.44
- Gadus-morrhua — 2.20
- Gmelina arborea — 4.30
- Hemidesmus indicus — 1.1
- Hypoprion brevirostris — 2.23
- Linum usitatisimum — 2.10, 2.12

- Moschus moschiferus — 1.48
- Nardastachys jatamansi — 1.15
- Nyctanlhus arbortristis — 4.27
- Ocimum sanctum — 1.39
- Olea europoea — 2.14
- Ovis aries — 2.25
- Piper longum — 1.23, 1.29
- Piper nigrum — 1.21
- Plantago ovata — 3.1
- Plantago psyllum — 3.3
- Plumbago zeylanica — 4.8
- Pongamia glabra — 2.8
- Ricinus communis — 2.3
- Santalum album — 1.4
- Saussurea costus — 4.6
- Saussurea lappa — 4.16
- Semicarpus anacardium — 2.1
- Sesamum indicum — 2.16
- Sida cordifolia — 4.3
- Theobroma cacao — 2.6
- Viola odorata — 4.6
- Vitex nirgundo — 1.28
- Wood fordia fruiticosa — 4.12
- Zingiber officinale — 1.34

# SYNONYM INDEX

| | | | |
|---|---|---|---|
| Adeps lanae | 1.71 | Marking nut | 1.52 |
| Aranya jirka | 1.102 | Moschus | 1.78 |
| Bahu mangiri | 1.6 | Mountain nard | 1.8 |
| Bdellium | 1.40 | Musk root | 1.8 |
| Benne oil | 1.67 | Nardus root | 1.8 |
| Bhutaghni | 1.6 | Night jasmine | 1.111 |
| Bibba | 1.52 | Nirgudi | 1.31 |
| Bitter apple | 1.44 | Oleum morrhi | 1.73 |
| Bitter cucumber | 1.44 | Oleum selachoids | 1.76 |
| Black pepper | 1.28 | Pepper | 1.28 |
| Boswellia | 1.34 | Pimpali | 1.4 |
| Cacao butter | 1.58 | Pipali | 1.4 |
| Colocynth pulp | 1.44 | Sallai guggul | 1.34 |
| Costus | 1.93 | Sallai-qum | 1.34 |
| Country mallow | 1.96 | Sariva | 1.1 |
| Cyperons nut guard | 1.23 | Shewan | 1.99 |
| Dhayati | 1.82 | Silabheda | 1.84 |
| Embelia | 1.11 | Sulabha | 1.6 |
| Flax seed | 1.61 | Surasa | 1.6 |
| Gambhari | 1.99 | Sweet flag | 1.25 |
| Garlic | 1.15 | Sweet violet | 1.50 |
| Gingelly oil | 1.67 | Sweet work wood | 1.114 |
| Ginger | 1.37 | Tamra pushpa | 1.82 |
| Gramya | 1.6 | Teel oil | 1.67 |
| Gugal | 1.40 | Tej patta | 1.18 |
| Gum guagal | 1.40 | Theobroma oil | 1.58 |
| Haldi | 1.46 | Turmeric | 1.46 |
| Honey | 1.80 | Vanjiraka | 1.102 |
| Indian beech | 1.54 | Vergin olive oil | 1.65 |
| Indian olibanum tree | 1.34 | White lead wart | 1.104 |
| Indian Saffron | 1.46 | White sandars | 1.20 |
| Indian Sarsaparilla | 1.1 | White teak | 1.99 |
| Indian Spikenand | 1.8 | Wild violet | 1.50 |
| Isabgol | 1.109 | Winter begonia | 1.84 |
| Ispaghula | 1.106 | Yellow bees wax | 1.69 |
| Jotishmati | 1.87 | Yellow nail dye paint | 1.90 |
| Kasturi | 1.78 | Yellow Sandars | 1.20 |
| Lanolin | 1.71 | Zangiber | 1.37 |
| Linum | 1.61 | Zingeberis | 1.37 |
| Margosa | 1.109 | | |

# CHEMICAL INDEX

| | | | |
|---|---|---|---|
| β-amyrin | 1.2 | Christembine | 1.13 |
| α-amyrine | 1.2 | Chrysophenol-D | 1.32 |
| α-asarone | 1.26 | Citranone | 1.105 |
| β-asurone | 1.26 | Comprene | 1.41 |
| β-Boswellic acid | 1.35 | Cucurbitecin E | 1.45 |
| α-cyperone | 1.23 | Curcumin | 1.48 |
| α-elaterin | 1.45 | Cyperene | 1.23 |
| α-santalol | 1.21 | d-Costen | 1.94 |
| β-santalol | 1.21 | Delta-7-avena sterol | 1.103 |
| β-sellinene | 1.23 | Demanolide Lactone | 1.103 |
| β-sitosterol | 1.2, 1.48, 1.55, 1.82, 1.100 | DHA | 1.74 |
| | 1.105, 1.109, 1.112 | Dihydro jatamansin | 1.9 |
| α-zingeberene | 1.38 | Elliptone | 1.105 |
| Acorone | 1.26 | Embelin | 1.13 |
| Ajone | 1.16 | Embelinol | 1.13 |
| Alenolenic acid | 1.48 | Embeliol | 1.13 |
| Allicin | 1.16 | EPA | 1.74 |
| Allin | 1.16 | Eugenol | 1.7 |
| Anguside | 1.32 | Fructose | 1.80 |
| Arbortristoside A | 1.113 | Furanogermenone | 1.18 |
| Arbortristoside B | 1.113 | Gallicin | 1.85 |
| Aricubin | 1.32 | Germacranolide | 1.103 |
| Artemisin | 1.115 | Gmelinoside | 1.100 |
| Artemisinin | 1.114 | Granulated honey | 1.81 |
| Astragaline | 1.112 | Guggulosterol-I | 1.41 |
| Azadiractin | 1.110 | Guggulusterone-Z | 1.41 |
| Barlerinoside | 1.91 | Hecogenin | 1.82 |
| Bergenin | 1.85 | Hemidesminine | 1.2 |
| Betaine | 1.97 | Hypapherine | 1.97 |
| Bhilawanol | 1.53 | Inulin | 1.94 |
| B-phenethylamine | 1.97 | isovanilline | 1.2 |
| Campesterol | 1.100 | Jatamansic acid | 1.9 |
| Carnanabic acid | 1.71 | Jatamansinol | 1.9 |
| Carotene | 1.112 | Jatamansone | 1.9 |
| Carvacrol | 1.7 | Karanjin | 1.55 |
| Caryophyllin | 1.7 | l-Costen | 1.94 |
| Celastrine | 1.88 | Linamarin | 1.62 |
| Centratherin | 1.103 | Linase | 1.62 |
| Cerotic acid | 1.70 | Linolein | 1.66 |
| Cholecalciferol | 1.75 | Lupeol | 1.2 |
| Cholesterol | 1.74 | Luteolin | 1.100 |

| | | | |
|---|---|---|---|
| Malic acid | 1.7 | Psorealin | 1.105 |
| Mardostachona | 1.9 | Querecetin | 1.82, 1.100, 1.110 |
| Mericyl palmitate | 1.70 | Qurecetol | 1.13 |
| Methyl eugenol | 1.7 | Ricinoleic acid | 1.57 |
| Methyl salicylate | 1.42 | Rutine | 1.51 |
| Muskone | 1.78 | Sarsapogenin | 1.2 |
| Myricin | 1.70 | Selenium | 1.16 |
| Nardostachyn | 1.9 | Serratol | 1.35 |
| Naringenin | 1.82 | Sesamin | 1.68 |
| Nictanthic acid | 1.112 | Sesamol | 1.68 |
| Nimbin | 1.110 | Sesamolin | 1.68 |
| Nimbolide | 1.109 | Shogaol | 1.38 |
| Nyctagenic | 1.112 | Squalene | 1.63 |
| Odoratine | 1.51 | Stigmesterol | 1.48 |
| Oleanolic acid | 1.112 | Sugeonol | 1.23 |
| Olein | 1.66, 1.68 | Tellurium | 1.16 |
| Omega-3-fatty acid | 1.48, 1.63 | Turmerone | 1.48 |
| p-caryophyllene | 1.19 | Valeranal | 1.9 |
| Peniculatin | 1.88 | Vasicinol | 1.97 |
| Piperidine | 1.29 | Vilangin | 1.13 |
| Piperine | 1.4, 1.29 | Violine | 1.51 |
| Piplasterol | 1.4 | Vit. A | 1.74, 1.77 |
| Piplertine | 1.4 | Vit. D | 1.74 |
| Plumbagic acid | 1.105 | Vit. $D_3$ | 1.75 |
| Plumbagin | 1.105 | Wood fordin A | 1.82 |
| p-methoxy salicylic aldehyde | 1.2 | Zingerone | 1.38 |
| Prioniside A | 1.91 | | |
| Prioniside B | 1.91 | | |

☛ ☛ ☛

www.ingramcontent.com/pod-product-compliance
Lightning Source LLC
Chambersburg PA
CBHW080824020726

47501CB00009B/2417